The Lorette Wilmot Library
Nazareth College of Rochester

DEMCO

Forbidden Fruit

and

Other Stories

Pablo La Rosa

Arte Público Press
Houston, Texas
1996

Acknowledgements of previously published work:

"Seagrapes" and "The Volunteer" originally appeared in *Kansas Quarterly*.

"El Comunista" originally appeared in *New Letters*.

"Chronicle of the Argonaut Pentapus" and the Spanish version of "The Death of Marielito" originally appeared in *The Americas Review*.

"Steppes" originally appeared in the anthology, *Paradise Lost or Gained: The Literature of Hispanic Exile*, published by Arte Público Press.

―∰

This volume is made possible through grants from the National Endowment for the Arts (a federal agency) and the Andrew W. Mellon Foundation.

Recovering the past, creating the future

Arte Público Press
University of Houston
Houston, Texas 77204-2090

Cover design by Susan Barber

La Rosa, Pablo
    Forbidden fruit and other stories / by Pablo
La Rosa.
        p.   cm.
    ISBN 1-55885-097-X
    1. Manners and customs—Fiction. I. Title.
PS3562.A7273F67   1996
813'.54—dc20   96-37665
                                                    CIP

To the memory of my father,
who told great stories.

To my mother and sisters,
who listened to the stories with me.

And to my wife and children,
who are the real story.

To Peter "Pedro" and Edna Stites,
whose invitation changed my life
more than they could have imagined.

Special thanks to my student assistant,
Shawn Wisley, for his help in preparing
the manuscript.

Contents

Forbidden Fruit

and

Other Stories

The Death of Marielito

I'm the one, I'm the one who must tell the story, write his mother in the barrio Buena Vista, municipality of Marianao, city of Havana, Cuba *Territorio Libre de America* and convey to her this infinitely deep, recurring sorrow that is circular like the bars of a blues. I must inform you that your son lies buried next to his son, your grandson, in a nameless grave of the Lincoln cemetery for poor blacks, City of Kansas, county of Jackson, state of Missouri, dead from a knife wound that ripped through his left lung and emptied all the pain from his heart just as he predicted, the man who kills me will be a fellow Cuban and he will attack from behind, no one dares take me on face to face, history repeats itself Chano Pozo, farewell my soul brother, farewell.

I am a piece of shit, all I'm good for is plagiarizing reality from one language to another (beware of the bilingual man, for he sucks with a forked tongue), reporting events without being a participant. I saw it coming and did nothing to prevent his suicide, because ever since his son—your grandson—died, he was pursuing it—death that is—chasing it like a fearless crusader in the back alleys of the vice-ridden rectangle bounded by Main-Linwood-39th. St.-Main: challenging two or three hoodlums at a time, laughing in the face of the toughest pimp, fucking whores without paying them, mugging nickle-and-dime crack dealers until Angola's woman got hot for him and took him to live with her while Angola finished serving the sentence for his latest burglary. Angola got wind of his woman's infidelity from a Mariel entering the slammer and sent a message through another Mariel who was being released—as soon as I'm out on the street you're dead, though we did time together in Guanajay and are brothers in exile I can't forgive this betrayal. You know very well what kind of a man I am, and that in Cuba I killed to pay back for a slap in the face—to which your son replied for Angola to think about it from all angles, that a bitch like her wasn't worth a death. And that if he, Angola, killed him, he'd solve nothing because they would either put him away for life at the Atlanta pen or make him sit in the electric chair, because in this country blacks convicted of murder are fried like pork rind, and that, in either case, that slut would go on giving booty to anyone she pleased in exchange for a nickle joint or a dime rock.

Angola was so pissed by your son's answer, he didn't wait out the remaining two months of his sentence. Taking advantage of the fact he's half Pugmy, he crawled into a ventilation shaft and made his escape on a moonless night, his soul horny for revenge. He stopped by their dump and, finding no one, grabbed a knife and headed straight for the *Who Cares-So What*, the dive on 39th and Troost where the Marieles gather nightly to drown their sorrows—the same place where a few months ago a teenage mother traded her newborn for twenty dollars' worth of crack. I have no doubt, ma'am, that you won't have any trouble understanding that the name of this bar (loosely translated), the *Qué carajo importa—Qué mas da*, captures the essence of the utter despair felt by the ghetto dwellers of Kansas City, be they black Americans or Marielitos of any shade of skin. Your son, as far as I know, did not frequent this joint before his son's death, but after that misfortune, he drifted there most nights after work. Sure enough, Angola caught him dancing with his woman and charged, knife cocked above his head. Angola didn't even scream, didn't call out your son's name; he simply grabbed him from behind and plunged the blade to the hilt. Pititi, a fellow from Matanzas who was present, told me the stab was so accurate your son collapsed instantly. By the time the ambulance arrived fifteen minutes later (because distress calls from the ghetto are not answered very promptly), all his bitterness, his endless unhappiness, and his life had coagulated on the filthy floor of the *Who Cares-So What*.

I want you to know, ma'am, that your son was not a bad sort, though he couldn't exactly be called an angel, since I understand one doesn't do time in Guanajay for petty offenses. He never did explain why he was doing 20 years when Fidel screwed Jimmy Carter by sending all those convicts and other undesirables who were contaminating his socialist utopia. But I can assure you that your son was not guilty of any of the brutal crimes that have given Marielitos here in Kansas City their well deserved bad reputation. You see, being a bilingual Cuban of the first generation (the *good* Cubans, the brave ones who fought in the Bay of Pigs, not the pigs from Mariel), I'm paid $30 per hour by the Municipal Court to cleave my tongue and make it chatter in both languages as an interpreter for my hapless countrymen. In this capacity I've seen incredible and horrendously bloody crimes—the man who killed his wife and his two-year old son with a .12-gauge blast because he thought she was coming on to another man at a dance sponsored by the Cuban-American Association of Kansas City; another who stabbed his former fiancée eighteen times on her birthday (one "candle for each year of her life," he boasted) because she had dumped him. Or the man from Santiago de Cuba who shoved a knife up a prostitute's rectum because she had stolen his wallet. (I know that Jack the Ripper used to slash vaginas, but buttholes!) Then, I've come across some cases that are laughable. A while back, for instance, they brought in a gay couple who had fought because one had cheated. The jealous party attacked his lover with a

knife, inflicting on him a superficial shoulder wound. It was
clear he could have killed his lover had he wanted to, but he
merely wished to teach him a lesson. The judge, after sentenc-
ing him to three months in jail for domestic violence, asked
me to explain to Seraphim (I swear that was his name) that in
this society we don't solve disputes with blades as is done in
backward cultures. Seraphim thought about it long and hard.
His answer, apparently quite sincere, left me speechless. I
could not force my prosthetic tongue to articulate the sylla-
bles. The brain had processed the translation successfully, but
the words were logjammed against the dam formed by my
throat. "Tell the judge," Seraphim instructed me, "that's
because in Cuba we can't get handguns as easily as one can
here." The judge tacked on three months to the sentence for
contempt of court.

I met your son in court. His case was more of a tragicome-
dy, with much to laugh and to cry about. Imagine, he was
charged with stealing several clothing items from the Salvation Army store on Main. Just in case you are not aware, it's a
second-hand shop where things discarded by the rich are sold
to the poor for nothing: shirts for 50 cents, pants for a buck,
winter coats for five, electric irons for two. Your son was
accused of smashing the window and taking a bag full of
clothes plus a crummy toaster. You must understand that, for
most Americans, to steal from the Salvation Army is like mugging Jesus Christ himself. The judge was fuming. He wanted
to know exactly what happened, and your son explained that
on his way home from work late one night, he walked past the
store and noted the display window was cracked. Since the
store's purpose was to help the poor and he was poor, he saw
no harm in reaching in and taking a bundle of panties. His
girlfriend was menstruating, he explained, and the few
panties she owned were bloodstained. I was so embarrassed to

translate his explanation in front of the ladies in attendance that I approached the judge and whispered it in his ear. The judge glanced at your son with a disgusted look and declared that in this case, the stolen goods themselves mattered little, that he was willing to let him go on parole on condition your son agreed to pay for the broken window. It was then I realized your son was different. He insisted he had smashed no window, and he wasn't paying to replace it. The lawyer and I advised him to accept the judge's deal, but he refused and was sentenced to thirty days at the county farm by his Highness.

I didn't see your son until about a year later, which was unusual because, as I told you, Marielitos have made themselves quite at home in court. This time they had nabbed him for warning two men that the woman flirting with them on the corner of Linwood and Main was no streetwalker, but an undercover agent posing as a prostitute. Your son had observed several unsuspecting victims fall for the trap and became incensed that the law would resort to such cheap tricks to deceive citizens. By means of gestures and using his broken English, he scared the men about to seal an agreement to have their cocks sucked away from the decoy's claws. The men took off like rockets down Linwood and escaped the hands of in(justice), but the policewoman summoned a paddy wagon on her walkie-talkie, and your son was carried off to the station.

The day of the hearing, the court-appointed lawyer advised him to make up a story, to say that he knew the two gentlemen and was simply greeting them. But he refused, arguing that in the land of the free the police has no business arresting a man simply because he wants a head job; that that was to be expected in a Communist country such as Cuba, where one has to ask Castro for permission even to fart. Meanwhile the judge was wanting to know what he was say-

ing, and I had to censor the last comment to spare him an
extra month in the can for contempt. Even so, the judge fined
him $100. But since he couldn't pay it, he was ordered to
spend a week at the farm. Your son made such a good impression on me that for the first time in my job as an interpreter I
offered to bail a Marielito out. He thanked me but refused my
offer to him; he explained the farm was a luxury hotel—he
was familiar with it; the food was fair; he could play baseball,
basketball, or pool; and either watch TV or the movies they
showed. What was a week at the county farm when he had
done ten hard years in Cuba, starving and getting whipped
until they let him flee to the U.S. once he signed a document
acknowledging he was not a political prisoner? He asked me,
though, for $5 for cigarettes for that week, and I gave it to
him gladly. I also gave him my phone number so he could call
me if he felt like having a beer after his release.

I must confess to you, ma'am, that I did it more for my
benefit than for his. Let me tell you a bit about myself. My
family got me out of Cuba in '59, and after a long process of
acculturation to the Anglo-Saxon way of life during which I
repressed all remnants of what I came to consider an inferior
culture, I surprised myself by dreaming about my childhood
and what I had left behind back in the Pearl of the Antilles.
All this after rejecting my Cuban citizenship, pledging alle-
giance to the balding eagle, marrying a WASP, having three
gringo children, who disappointed me by not being blond, and
living in the geo-moral heart of this contradictory nation.
Once in a while I visited Miami in an attempt to expose my
Cuban roots. But I always returned to Kansas City dejected,
feeling all the more alienated—more distant from my family,
my countrymen—and realizing I could never be a true American no matter how much I wanted it. Dreams provided some
comfort while they lasted, but my anguish became greater

when all I could recall were fragments of that past. It was
about that time I started smoking pot—if the Court should
find out they would strip me of my job, my citizenship, my
children even—and discovered that if I shut myself in my
study to listen to Afro-Cuban music stoned, I could pretend I
was back in my hometown. Believe me, at times the illusion
was so real it left me wondering. Where was I? Lying under
the almond tree in Varadero or on the floor of my study in
Kansas City, tuned in to Santana's "La fuente del ritmo"? My
friend Kent, a Mormon mystic, assured me I was in fact trans-
ported in body and soul to the world of my childhood. Didn't I
see my own limp body sprawling lifeless on the floor? That
was proof enough of the miracle. My wife, on the contrary,
determined I was becoming neurotic and demanded I stop
smoking. I had to comply because my son had noticed my
strange behavior and had asked about the strange odor coming out of dad's study when he listened to his records.

If you don't have butter, you gotta use margarine. I saw
the Marielitos as a source of information that could help me
fill those voids in the collective memory that drove me nuts.
But the people from Immigration had recommended I avoid
befriending them, a piece of advice that seemed reasonable
considering the atrocities they were responsible for. But your
son's behavior in court, plus the tragicomic nature of his purported crimes, gave me an excuse to end the blockade. It was
one of the few decisions in my life I have not come to regret.

I know, ma'am, that you must have suffered terribly
because of your son, but you can rest your conscience because
he always spoke of you with affection and respect. You are not
to blame. I know you always warned him not to stray from the
narrow path, and that, as Cubans say, *"Chivo que rompe tam-
bor con su pellejo lo paga"* (The goat who tears up a drum has
to pay for it with his own skin.). According to him, his misfor-

tune was the fault of the goddam streets, where you learn all that is evil. What else could you have done all alone with so many children but what you did? Give them good advice and let them roam the streets of Havana to try to make a dime. Teach them to hang on to the instinct for survival the African slaves brought to the New World, the same instinct that led him to father a child here in spite of the unfavorable conditions.

When your son finally called me several weeks after the hearing to have a beer, I was delighted because I thought he either had forgotten or didn't want to befriend me. I remember the day well: a sparkling, crisp autumn afternoon, the best time of year in the Midwest. I crossed the Missouri, a wide river that now serves as a barrier between the ghetto and the white suburbs to the north. Needless to say, I had driven through the ghetto often, but always using the superhighway or well-lit, well-guarded avenues. Until that day, I had never set foot on a street inhabited by blacks. I must admit that, had your son not been waiting for me on the steps to his building, I'd have kept on driving.

No, ma'am, I never got to go inside a tenement in Havana, but they couldn't be as depressing as these apartment houses here. Poverty is one thing, but these ghetto areas stand for something much worse, that who-cares-so-what attitude. The sign Dante found at the entrance to Hell has the same meaning. We're talking about a life with no hope. Without being a sociologist, I can see why broken glass—odd pieces of an unworkable puzzle—is so abundant in the ghetto.

You probably would like to know how your son wound up there. Well then. The Marielitos convicted of crimes in Cuba, like him, are transferred from federal prisons to so-called halfway houses (half slammer, half heartbreak hotel) so they can begin to learn to function, under supervision, in this alien society, get a job, and pay taxes—to relieve the overburdened American taxpayer who is saddled with the upkeep of unwanted immigrants. Once they find a job, they are let loose, even though it is obvious they are not ready to succeed by legal means in an economy based on Spencerian Darwinism. Since most can't speak, read, or write English, the only jobs they find are as dishwashers or busboys, and the little money they earn is not enough for them to rent a decent apartment.

Your son ended up at a complex. It was subsidized by the city (located on 31st and Campbell, smack in the middle of the cocaine trade). Suffice it to say that as soon as I stepped out of my car, two black teenagers tried to push $5 rocks on me, because as your son explained, the only white folks who wander through those parts are addicts looking to score. It was in that "project," as subsidized housing is called in this country, that your son met the girlfriend who had the menstrual blood-stained panties.

She had been born and raised in projects such as this one. Before moving in with your son, she lived with her paraplegic mother and countless brothers, sisters, nephews, and nieces of all ages. Her father had died years before; he'd been an alcoholic who used to beat the shit out of her mother (that explains why she was a paraplegic) and the kids until one night the older brother fought back and killed him with a hammer. Maybe you can't believe the story, but I swear it is true. After your grandson died, I did a thorough investigation of the family, because I am convinced (and your son shared in the feeling) that the baby didn't die of natural causes as stated in the death certificate; no, ma'am. The only way to begin to understand why the young mother killed her son, though she cannot be forgiven, is to know the history of her family.

I am absolutely certain, ma'am, that your son didn't love her, but you will understand that here winters are hellish and that his loneliness had to rival that of a runaway slave. With this woman, he had at least a chunk of human flesh to embrace during the night, and what's to be expected happened. She got pregnant. That fall afternoon when I met her, the pregnancy was already quite evident. Ma'am, your blood and that of your ancestors, through your son, was about to grow roots in a land totally different from the African or Cuban savannah. Yet your son was proud that his woman was pregnant. He chose a name for the child who would bear his seed: Mariel. He was sure it was a boy. He wanted to honor the infamous harbor from which he'd sailed to his alleged freedom.

I often sought him out during the following months. Listening to him speak made my day. He turned out to be the informant of my dreams. Hearing his voice, my maternal tongue regained its lost elasticity; fragments scattered about my memory coalesced in sharper, truer-to-life images than those I had conjured up smoking dope. Through his words I lived the triumphant hours of Playa Girón, the anguish-filled days of October, his forced participation in the Ten Million Harvest. Through his songs I felt the joy of street rumbas, the laughter stirred by the carnival conga chants protesting rationing—give us chicken, give us bread, but above all give us panties to cover our buns.

His comments also opened my eyes to life in the United States. First of all, he'd say, that it was undeniable that Americans had plenty of money, but that they lacked heart. The reverse was true of the Russians. It was beyond his comprehension why so much was spent building highways instead of housing for the poor. He had also developed some thought-provoking theories that chicken here was synthetic because, as long as he'd been in this country, he'd never seen a live one, and because it was impossible to raise enough chickens to supply so many Kentucky Frieds. By the same token, he'd argue how was it possible to raise enough cattle to make the billions of hamburgers sold at McDonald's, which led him to the conclusion that they were a mixture of beef, plastic, and asphalt.

Months went by, and before you knew it the baby was born. Your son telephoned me from the hospital with the news and to ask me to interpret for him, because there was trouble and he didn't understand the nurses. I admit I went grudgingly. It was rather late and extremely cold. They were at Truman Medical, the hospital for the uninsured, in other words, the black ghetto population. He was waiting in the lobby, and I could tell he was very upset. We went up to the maternity ward where he pointed to a squirmish, skin-and-bones baby in an incubator tagged "Baby Jones"; since they weren't married, it had been given the mother's maiden name. The baby had come two months prematurely; it barely weighed four and a half pounds and it had a tube inserted in every opening of its undersize body.

The nurse on duty walked over and explained the baby had the symptoms of a crack baby. What this meant, ma'am, was that the mother was addicted to cocaine and had given the addiction to the critter. I was stunned because your son hadn't told me his woman did cocaine. I asked him if he smoked it as well, but he denied it. He had tried it once and realized drugs can only lead to death. That to get it you either kill or get killed. But all her brothers were users, and although he beat her on several occasions in an attempt to make her stop, it was easy for her to feed her vice when he was at work.

After a week in the hospital, all the tubes were disconnected from the infant. Mother and child were sent packing because they needed the incubator for another baby suffering from the same conditions. When I paid them a visit at the apartment the following weekend, I could see the baby was a bundle of nerves. It was constantly whimpering. Your son would pick him up and rock him with tenderness, but it scared me to see that the mother didn't want anything to do with the baby; she stayed glued to the TV screen as if nothing else existed. She couldn't even nurse her son because the doctors said her milk was contaminated. In other words, she showed no maternal instincts. Your son was the one who washed and boiled the bottles, warmed the welfare formula, and fed him. It was your son who changed the diapers when Marielito soiled them.

He didn't live a month. One morning around 2 a.m., the call from your son rescued me from one nightmare only to sink me in another one from which there was no escape. He was in jail. Choking, he told me that when he got home from washing dishes after midnight, he'd found the baby crumpled in the crib and his woman in a stupefied state in front of the television. Convinced that she had strangled or asphyxiated the baby because his constant crying drove her crazy, he beat her with all his strength and would have killed her if her brothers, who live on the same floor, hadn't stopped him.

At first, the police suspected your son had strangled the baby. Had that been the case, I'm certain he'd have been sent to the chair, given the fact he was a Marielito. But when they sorted things out and determined who was the guilty party, the autopsy report blamed the death on that mysterious plague that claims so many black children's souls in the ghetto, crib death. You see, to send a mother to prison for life for killing her baby costs the state hundreds of thousands of dollars, and besides, the death of a black baby is not a loss to society but rather a great savings in welfare costs. So who cares if a black mother kills her black child.

I wish, ma'am, I could tell you a different story; tell you that your son made it to the promised land, and that, like myself, he had good luck, learned English, found a decent job, married a good wife, and fathered three children who would succeed in this brave new world. But reality is as bitter and murky as the thick coffee I've been shooting all night long. Without a doubt Charlie Parker swallowed acid on nights like this which he'd later vomit through his burning saxophagus. But I can't sing the blues to unload this deep sorrow. I can only harmonize my inner weeping with the slow, icy rain that began falling hours ago, and pour my pain onto this letter that I can't finish because it is about a circular and recurring sorrow like the bars of a blues tune. History repeats itself. Farewell, my soul brother, farewell.

Sergeant Sugar

In Cuba you were born with your basic reflexes plus one that was just as critical for survival: fear of the police. Whether the uniform was the foreboding blue of the city cop or the ominous khaki of the regular army, your natural reaction was to freeze upon spotting one. As a child, I witnessed the beating of a drunkard right at our doorsteps. He had refused to go home when commanded. The policeman drew his nightstick and clubbed the man until the poor bastard fell unconscious to the ground. If my genes didn't carry fear of the uniform from centuries of Spanish oppression and decades of dictatorship, I assure you they mutated right then and there. To this day, after years of residence in the land of the free, I cannot help feeling guilty of some unspecified crime when I see a policeman. If I am driving, I slow down even though I am not speeding. When I go into a bank or an expensive store, I am uncomfortably aware of the guard's scrutiny. I cannot overcome this phobia; it is as indelible as my accent.

The chief of police in my hometown was a crude fellow who happened to be on the right side when Batista pulled his coup. As a reward for his loyalty, he was promoted to sergeant and given the job vacated by a man who supported the wrong politico in the power struggle. Since his name, Alzugaray, sounded like the Spanish word for sugar, he was dubbed Sergeant Sugar, a nickname that was doubly appropriate because he suffered from diabetes.

Sergeant Sugar was fond of riding in the back seat of his patrol car, a slick blue Oldsmobile from the new fleet Batista acquired for his henchmen. He rode slowly and systematically through town, instilling into every man, woman, and child the certainty that he was always looking over your shoulder. More than once the beam of his searchlight had exposed a young couple on the beach; more than once a warning blast from his siren had sent us scrambling after raiding Doctor Maribona's mango trees. Yes, he was omnipresent, omniscient and, like God, silent. When he had something to say to someone, he'd stay in the car and let his bodyguard do the talking.

A couple of years after Batista's coup, Fidel Castro landed in Oriente province with his ragtag rebels. Things got hot. Every day we heard rumors of attacks on army garrisons or police stations. Our town was small, isolated, and, by-and-large, peaceful. But Alzugaray took no chances. He posted sentries at headquarters around the clock. His bodyguard began toting a machine gun in addition to his sidearm.

One morning after a terrorist bomb blew up a power relay station, two men were found hanged on a *ceiba* tree a few kilometers inland. The bodies were brought to the town square, dumped in the middle, and exhibited for the entire day. Each had a cardboard sign strung around his neck with the words "por revolucionario" printed in deep red. The message was effective. In the three years of fighting, not another anti-government incident took place in our town. When people dared discuss the revolution, they whispered. The name Castro was unmentionable. No one could prove it, but all believed Sergeant Sugar had executed the hangings.

My father got me a surprise for my thirteenth birthday. He'd gone to Havana on business, and I expected a new watch or perhaps even a bicycle. But I was really thrilled to find a gun on my bed when I got home from school. I had used Aldo's BB gun on occasion, but this particular kind was a pellet model that proved powerful enough to consistently shatter bottles from a distance of thirty feet. It ripped lizards in two, as if they were made of papier-mâché, and gutted sparrows I shot for target practice as they groomed their feathers on the almond tree behind our house. I was really honing my aim and felt proud of its deadliness.

One afternoon I went over to an abandoned field that had quite a bit of unchecked growth. Some kids claimed they'd seen a big snake in the brush, and I wanted to test my new weapon on larger game. I combed the place for a good half-hour with no luck. I didn't want to go home empty-handed, so I decided to try to shoot one of those finches Columbus describes in his diary of the discovery of Cuba. Next to sparrows, these birds are diminutive and much more beautiful. Their chests are covered with a golden down and their wing tips are yellow-green. They never stand still for more than a second, so to hit one with a single pellet is difficult. After stalking for a good while under a tree, one finally landed and I bagged it.

As I came out of the field onto the dirt road, Sergeant Sugar was driving by. The Oldsmobile slowed, stopped, and the bodyguard motioned me over.

The inborn fear of the uniform seized me. My legs refused to move and my tongue froze. Realizing I wasn't going anywhere, Alzugaray's driver put the car in reverse and pulled up to where I stood. All I was conscious of was the black machine gun on the front seat.

"You shot that finch?" Sergeant Sugar asked.

His voice sounded as I imagined it would, thunderous and oligarchical.

I showed him where the pellet severed my trophy's neck.

"Good shooting."

"Thank you, sir." I stammered, feeling somewhat relieved.

"Are you going to eat it?"

"Oh no, sir. I'm going to bury it after I show it to my friends."

"Bury it? You mean you shoot birds for the hell of it?"

I searched for an answer, any answer, but I was too confused. I gave up.

"I guess so."

"You don't kill nothing for the hell of it, son. Let me have that gun. When you find a good reason, you come tell me, and maybe if I like it, maybe, you can have it back."

They drove off. I stood on the dirt road until the sun got so hot my eyes watered.

✺

Three days after Batista fled Cuba, the first rebels stormed into town in a captured Jeep. They were quite a sight with their long hair, matted beards and battered Springfields. First thing they wanted to know was where the chief of police might be hiding. A tip led them to the sacristy. After negotiating through the priest, Sergeant Sugar surrendered with the promise of fair play.

The trial was so swift they might as well had not held it. The mother of one of the hanged men pointed a finger at Alzugaray. That was all the evidence needed to convict him as a war criminal.

Though the execution was public, I didn't go. But I heard the description so many times I remember it as if I had been present.

They stripped him of his uniform. In plain white clothes, he seemed as vulnerable as any human being. His unshaven face enhanced the forlorn look in his dark eyes. His fleshy lips quivered as he was blindfolded. Two militiamen pushed him against the freshly whitewashed wall. The officer in charge asked the crowd once more if anyone objected to the execution.

Twenty feet away the three weathered Springfields were raised. A loud report, as if fired from a single rifle, and the wall became a bright canvas painted with blood.

El Comunista

I was old enough to tell right from wrong when my father ran for representative from the central district of the province of Matanzas. Being elected—or better yet, selected—for office was definitely the quickest way to riches in the rotten system. Although all candidates denounced the system's corruption as a matter of etiquette, there was no question that their eagerness to be public servants stemmed from a desire to serve themselves from the public trust. Of course there were risks involved (my father started packing a .38 the day he announced his candidacy), but the potential rewards overwhelmed the inherent dangers of Cuban politics. We the children were perfectly willing to forego a father for the chance to savor opulence, no matter how ephemeral it proved to be. We succumbed to the prospects of moving to one of those Italianate mansions politicians occupied in Havana's Avenue of the Presidents, which was just the appetizer of a tantalizing feast. There'd be late-model Cadillacs *avec* chauffeurs, membership to the exclusive Vedado Tennis Club, shopping sprees to New York and, if the party survived the push and shove for several years, a Chris Craft to complement the beach-front villa in idyllic Varadero. With luck, you would transfer enough of the national treasure to Miami banks for the inevitable day your patron dictator was overthrown and his entourage forced into exile by the new wave of plunderers.

Not that we were poor by Cuban standards. We had a live-in cook, a young mulatto woman from our farm who decided this type of bondage was more bearable than life in the cane fields, and we also employed the services of an asthmatic

teen-ager who scrubbed the tile floors daily for a few bucks a
month and regular lunches, something her brothers and sisters couldn't depend on. But we didn't own a car, could not
afford to attend prestigious schools where English was taught
to perfection, and my sisters whined that their clothes looked
like rags. We were extremely envious of our cousins (who
made sure we felt this way). We coveted the lifestyle they
flaunted when they came to visit. We in fact felt cheated by
fate because our father, unlike our uncles, had failed to preserve and multiply his share of the fortune handed down by
grandfather. After years of wallowing in the middle class, we
believed we deserved a sojourn in the aristocracy, and we perceived the elections not only as the means to this end, but perhaps as our last and only chance.

Politics was not new to my family. My grandfather had
risen to the rank of lieutenant in the war against Spain, and
he parlayed his military exploits into the mayor's office of our
small city. He eventually became the governor of Matanzas
and might have gone the distance to the Capitol if not for his
premature death. My father had a definite headstart thanks
to this legacy, but he lacked the financial resources to mount a
successful campaign. In a country and age where electronic
media was practically non-existent, candidates didn't waste
money on political messages. They went directly to the voters
and bought their votes.

It was our uncles' idea to have Father run for the Assem-
bly, and it was they who put up the capital. They claimed they
wanted to restore the family prestige in the political arena,
though in truth, they were more concerned with protecting
their privileges. As large landholders or *latifundistas*, they
feared the reformist talk of a young lawyer named Castro who
wanted to limit the size of farms to 1,000 acres. A brother in
the Capitol would go a long way toward abating those fears.

My father kicked off his campaign with a flamboyant speech, much too long for the savage heat, which the crowd endured because we were giving away several hundred pounds of rice and beans brought down from the farm. After the fanfare, my sisters and I stood behind the gunny sacks filling receptacles raised timidly by the hands of the town's poor. I felt strangely powerful as I determined how much rice each woman or child received. Surely we were meant to govern over these submissive people. According to Uncle Roberto, it was a simple matter of heredity; our genes were dominant.

Giving away food was a good publicity stunt, but it didn't guarantee votes. The only sure-fire method was to outbid your opponents for the right to mark a voter's ballot on election day. The scheme worked like this: You hired a canvasser from each of the most populous precincts. His job was to feel out the registered voters for their preference. If they weren't committed to a particular candidate, you recruited them to yours. On election day, the canvasser was among the first to vote, except he didn't mark his ballot. Instead, he stuffed it in his pocket and smuggled it outside. At a predetermined location, his recruits assembled. He gave one of them the ballot, now properly marked, and the recruit proceeded to the polling place. Upon presenting his registration, he was given a blank ballot and allowed inside the booth. He'd then drop the marked ballot in the box, put the blank one in his pocket, and return it to the canvasser, who'd pay him for it. Thus the chain began. It was crooked, but it worked.

As election day drew near, Father redoubled his campaign efforts. He was on the road constantly, and I was allowed to tag along on a few occasions. We'd pull into these one-street towns, horns blaring, wait for the people to gather around the loudspeaker mounted atop one of the cars, play a few cha-cha tunes to get them in a good mood, and spray nickels and dimes around like chicken feed. Father would then give a short speech, which he ended by promising that if elected, there'd be more for everyone, though he never specified more of what.

The canvassers' tally sheets were brimming with names. We were all excited except Mother, who was content with her lot and thought it was wrong to deny the will of God. But she was weak, and her opinion weightless. She shook her head as my sisters and I argued over the schools we'd attend in Havana, the color of the cars, the stores where we should shop. We were learning the lesson, and the lesson was that money could buy anything or anyone. No one seemed immune to the corruption. It was as if a moral malaria had infected the island, and the only way to control the fever was with a transfusion of bribes.

Father was upset when informed that Orestes Fundora had refused to pledge his ballot and the ballots of those he controlled to our cause. Orestes, whom everybody jokingly called "el comunista," was the most popular man in town. As the power company's lone employee, he was responsible for all aspects of the operation, from changing street lamps to collecting bills. His popularity was due to the fact that he didn't have the heart to shut anyone off and because he was the home team's baseball manager. His squads were the pride of a community that didn't have much to be proud of. No one could forget the time he inserted himself as a pinchhitter, at age 45, and whistled a bases-loaded double down the right-field line to beat the big boys from Santiago. The Communist label stuck to him after statements he made to the effect that electricity should be free for the poor. After all, he reasoned, most lived in one-room shacks with no other electrical appliance than a 25-watt bulb.

Father summoned *el comunista* to our house for a confer-
ence. Orestes arrived as we were finishing lunch, politely
exposed his balding head, and turned down an invitation to
sample Mother's guava marmalade. When we finished
dessert, Father ordered us to clear the dining room. Anxious
to learn first-hand how bribes worked, I went outside, circled
the house, and crawled into the hedge under the dining room
window. I had missed the formalities over coffee. I heard the
cook remove the demitasses and a cumbersome silence pre-
vailed.

"Cigar?" Father offered.

"No thank you."

I pictured Father biting off the end of his *H. Upmann
ExtraFino*, striking a match with gusto and taking several
deep draws. He'd then examine the advancing rings of ashes
with the satisfaction of someone who understands that the
Grand Scheme of Things is a Great Scam.

Father began by inquiring about the team's prospects for
the coming year. Orestes replied that it'd be tough to replace
his pitching ace Manolo, who had married and moved to
Matanzas City looking for work. His shortstop, Cheo, was
slowing down, couldn't go deep in the hole or lead off effective-
ly anymore. But Guaco showed a lot of promise; and if Rigo
learned to control his breaking pitch, they'd be competitive.

I knew Father didn't like baseball, but I could see his
strategy was working. At least it got Orestes talking.

Next, Father asked if I could start practicing with the
team. I was spending too much time with my sisters playing
sissy games; it'd do me good to be around men. Besides, he
wanted me to try out for my new school's squad when we
moved to Havana. Orestes wasn't thrilled, but he said it'd be
okay as long as I stayed in the outfield, away from the hot
shots.

It was time to bring up the real business of the meeting. There was a long pause during which Father must have chewed assiduously on his *H. Upmann*. Inside the bush, a chameleon unfurled its guttural membrane, did a set of pushups, and assumed the color of the branch, anticipating a victim.

"Fundora, after I win the elections I'll be in a prime position to help your team. Of course, I got to have a reason. Do you follow me?"

"Yes, sir."

"For example, we can start by getting every player new uniforms. Real uniforms, made in the U.S.A. Your men look like shit in those flour bags your wife sews. Shoes, too. I don't see how anyone can steal bases barefoot."

"You got a point there."

"We can also throw in bats, gloves, catching gear—you name it. Someday, we might even be able to build stands for your fans."

Fundora didn't answer. A red ant came crawling up the branch, and the chameleon devoured it as it got within range. So easy when you could change colors.

"How much did my opponent offer you, Orestes?"

"Five per vote."

"Is that all? Tell you what. You deliver me one-hundred ballots, and I'll match his offer as well. No need to tell anyone about the cash either. It's your compensation. You just tell the players and fans you need a hundred votes so your team can be the sharpest-looking in the Province of Matanzas."

I was impressed with the subtle progression of Father's offers. He had been able to camouflage the bribe without compromising Fundora's pride.

"You just tell your people to see Molina on election day. I guarantee you the equipment will be here before the season starts. Let's shake hands on the deal."

I heard the scraping of chairs against the tile. The buyout was about to be consummated, I thought.

"I can't do it," Fundora said.

"You drive a hard bargain, Orestes. You're tougher to deal with than I imagined. Here, take these hundred pesos as a gesture of my good faith. Go ahead, they don't bite!"

"I can't, sir. The way I see it, my men don't need uniforms. They can play barefoot. They can even play barehanded, but it's awfully hard to play on empty guts. We don't need handouts every four years, sir. We need a government that doesn't allow so many people to go hungry day after day."

My father exploded. I had witnessed his quick anger on plenty of occasions, but this time his voice burst with a terrifying rage.

"Fundora, I always thought your nickname was only a joke, but you talk like you believe that horseshit about equality."

"I just want the game of life to start like a game of baseball, sir. Zero to zero."

"Yeah, you *are* a goddam communist. You better watch your step, old man. They got these cozy little cells under Morro Castle reserved for your kind, if you're lucky enough to get there alive."

⁂

We never found out if Father was elected. Before the ballots could be counted, an Army commander named Fulgencio Batista declared the elections null and void, stormed the presidential palace, and decreed himself president. My uncles cried foul, my sisters cried, and I started swinging the bat at imaginary curve balls so I'd be ready in case Orestes called on me to pinch hit someday.

Chronicle of the Argonaut Pentapus

Of all the land and sea animals known to man, the polypus is perhaps one of the least understood and most needlessly feared by humans. A spineless, disproportionately large-headed creature with shifty eyes, the polypus prefers to scrape along the murky bottom and to hole up where light barely disturbs the darkness. But in spite of its menacing appearance, this cephalopod is a harmless being. It feeds with suckers hidden in the lower half of its tentacles; it entraps weaker life forms and takes them to a mouth equipped with a sharp, file-like tongue used to crush crustaceans, its favorite food. The polypus is not, therefore, the man-eating monster described in old mariners' and fishermen's tales. In truth, the polypus will avoid confrontations with superior adversaries, and when threatened or frightened, its skin changes color and it sprays jets of ink to blind the enemy and cover its retreat. It is, however, in the peculiar way the polypus copulates that our true nature is revealed with greatest clarity. This has been amply documented by a famous underwater explorer, the one who has filmed those incredible aquatic ejaculations, ranging from the foamy cascades of the sperm whale to the insoluble, oily droplets of the unfortunate crab.

I began to feel like a polypus a few days after I left my wife and children. At first I felt like an alienated octopus, if that makes any sense. I haven't counted how many suction cups we have, but after abandoning my family I had the sensation my tentacles had come unglued and that they were spinning wildly, like blades adrift in a sea of wind. My only support was my own body, flaccid and slippery. I am afraid a polypus can't survive long in such a helpless state.

This wasn't the first time I ran away. I had done it twice previously. But on both occasions I returned before a month elapsed begging forgiveness. Yet those brief excursions left a longing for freedom deep inside that neither wife nor children could quench. She blamed herself, but now I am convinced it'd have been the same with any other mate. After fertilization of the eggs, unlike its female counterpart who won't abandon the nest until the very last offspring has emerged from the embryonic stage, the male polypus continues his nomadic existence in the marine deserts, impregnating all willing females he finds along the way. But I can no longer fertilize egg clusters, for my semen is as sterile as the sands of the Dead Sea.

To help me remember who I am, or at least who I was a few months ago, I opened my passport to review the vital information. I still look entirely human in the photograph. My wife always claimed I have sneaky eyes, and she's right—I've never been able to look straight at a camera. Undeniably, my eyes are like those of a polypus, or, at the very least, like those of a squid.

I must have mutated greatly since the photo was taken. The first time I cashed traveler's checks, the clerk didn't pay any attention to my face; she merely compared the signatures on the checks to the one in the passport. But the very last time, the cashier made me endorse the checks front and back—he obviously was having difficulty reconciling the face on the document to the one facing him. Finally, he wrote down my passport number on a notebook and asked where I was staying. I gave him a fictitious hotel named after some obscure pre-Colombian ruins.

According to the visa stamp, I crossed the border a little over two months ago. I got paid on the first, and from the bank, I went straight to the bus station. I prefer this mode of transportation, not so much because it's cheap, but for the type of people that use it. It was actually in a bus where I met the female who taught me to use my hectocotylus in a primitive manner. But that was years ago, and I had no inkling then what was in the future.

After a forty-hour trip I arrived at the capital of this underdeveloped nation. I decided to come here because I can make my dollars stretch, and because in a few hours I could reach the sea if I so desired. (I've always felt a tremendous need to be near water and couldn't explain it until now.) However, the real reason I came here was so that I could immerse myself in a cultural déjà vu. Underdeveloped societies tend to imitate trends and fashions that were in vogue years before in the industrialized world, and I thought I might be able to take advantage of another sexual revolution. Until recently, though, I had the luck of a celibate monk.

It would appear from my experience here that homosexual liberation precedes the heterosexual revolution. I've been courted by gays since the day I arrived. They see me alone and conclude I must be gay, too. I've been asked to the movies, to dance, even been offered monetary rewards. I truly appreciate my suitors' brotherly love, but they must understand that we polypi are restricted to heterosexual copulation. In years past, I may have resented all their attention, considering it a threat to my masculinity, but now I welcome it, since gays are among the few who are not disgusted by my appearance.

Until the other day, the only women who didn't avoid me were the beggars. Not even prostitutes came near me. I was desperate; my suction cups sucked on one another for lack of a strange body on which to find support. I visited anthropologi-

cal museums, modern art museums, the avant-garde book-
stores where one should find those trail-blazing females of the
erotic revolution, but I didn't make contact. Either there are
none in this country, or they are sill in the underground
phase.

Finally, I met her one afternoon. I am a romantic polypus,
so I believe in fate. I was at an outdoor cafe pretending to read
a poetry journal when I had a feeling. I looked up exactly at
the moment she looked at me. She stopped as if to read the
menu posted at the entrance and then sat at the table next to
mine very naturally. She ordered a cappuccino, and I kept
pretending I was reading my magazine. At last I got tired of
the game and simply asked her if she was traveling alone, for
obviously she too was foreign. We talked for a good hour. My
vocal cords hurt, I thought, because I hadn't had a sustained
conversation in weeks. Now I know it's because I'm losing my
ability to speak.

Not only my voice. My mental faculties are faltering, and
along with them, language itself. I close my eyes and I see
submerged landscapes, the skeletons of sunken galleons in the
Sea of the Antilles, or Ionic amphora that once upon a time
gave me shelter in the Mediterranean or Red Seas. I fear that
soon I will cease to be human altogether and won't be able to
use the ink from my glands to finish this chronicle.

That night I couldn't sleep. I was brutally frank and
asked her to spend the night with me. She thought about it
briefly, but denied my request, claiming she was very tired.
However, she said, she'd like to see me the next day. I went to
her hotel at first light. The night clerk didn't allow me to go
up to her room. He phoned her instead, and while I waited, he
didn't take his eyes off me. When she at long last came down
to the lobby, I grabbed her hand and led her to a nearby park.
I told her everything—that I was married with children, that I

was desperate, that I believed I was turning into a polypus. When I finished my confession, she stroked my hair and sank into deep thought. Then her blue eyes came to life and she said: "I have an idea. Let's leave for the coast this afternoon. We can get better acquainted by the sea."

My thoughts are becoming more and more incoherent as my mind gets into an extremely desultory mode. It must be apparent, because people eye me with fear and even street vendors go out of their way to avoid me. Since she disappeared, I hardly leave the hotel room. I step out only to quench this thirst for sea water that burns my insides and to take my midday seafood meal at a bay-side restaurant. At night I lie awake thinking until very late, so late the only noise to be heard is that of the rats and the waves eating away the foundations of the port. I go into the bathroom to be surprised by the mirror. I catch a glimpse of a shocked, unrecognizable face that doesn't match the memory I have of myself, because I've been evolving in reverse and what I was years or months ago has no resemblance to what I am now. I turn out the lights and spend an eternity sucking on the sheet's edge. Then I am overwhelmed by desire. I would masturbate into oblivion if not for the fact that we polypi can't masturbate, all the tentacles notwithstanding. Besides, I lost my hectocotylus and I must wait for another to grow.

I wonder how long that might take. I fear that this cavity may be permanent, leaving me a polyped eunuch for the rest of my new life; that this coagulated mass of blood vessels might not be able to decipher the genetic code for hectocotylus regeneration, and that my pentatentacle has been irreplaceably lost to the treacherous female. She lured me to the sea so I could impregnate her, but she didn't know a surgeon removed my seminal vessels the day after my last offspring was born. She's probably holed up in a ledge of the continental shelf, awaiting futilely the birth of thousands of our offspring.

We made the bus trip in silence. She fell asleep on my shoulder, and I had to keep touching her to make sure it all wasn't a dream. Throughout the ride I had the impression I was a silent-movie spectator, that the landscape of volcanic rocks and malnourished fields was only an illusion projected on the window. As we approached the coastal plain, my skeleton softened. Each time a whiff of saltpeter-laden breeze seared my nostrils, my body tissue thinned. When I saw the ocean in the distance, I understood this was a journey with no return. I must have trembled, for she awoke and caressed me.

We caught a taxi, and I asked the driver to take us to a second-class hotel with a beach front. On the register form I marked we were married, but I could tell the clerk didn't believe it from her sardonic smile. I asked for a room with natural ventilation, with a balcony overlooking the ocean. The clerk insisted I pay in advance, after remarking sarcastically that air-conditioned rooms weren't that expensive.

We spent three days in an agonizing apprenticeship. I believed I made love rather competently. But my method was human, and she had to teach me the way polypi mate. As soon as the bellhop had left us alone in our room, I had embraced her violently and tried to kiss her on the neck. She rejected my overtures, and this really confused me. I looked at her right in the eyes, begging for an explanation. I had thought we wouldn't be wasting time on childish psychological foreplay.

"I get more pleasure from a warm bath than from making love with a man," she said.

I answered I didn't understand.

"I mean that most men make love as if they were racing. They struggle so hard to cross the finish line first."

I felt ashamed. Her words made certain lightning-quick copulations from my youth come to mind.

"Forget it, it's not your fault. Undress."

We undressed without touching. I was accustomed to having to undress the female as a prerequisite to lovemaking, and it took great effort to hold back. She instructed me to sit at one end of the bed, and she took a yoga position on the opposite side. We looked at each other for over an hour. The sun was setting, and the constant crash of the waves was hypnotizing. I watched as her skin changed hues. Two red circles grew around her eyes. My body started moving towards her. Our tentacles met cautiously at first; then mine explored her supple cephalopod body and we became one. I felt her abdomen open under mine, allowing the hectocotylus to penetrate fully. We remained motionless for a very long time. When we separated, the sun had set hours before.

I turned on the lights. She had returned to her human form. I looked in the mirror with horror, but I too had regained the body of a man. We dressed and went out on the streets, sharing an unspeakable secret. We hadn't eaten since morning and were famished. We found an outdoor restaurant and chose a table sheltered from the bustle. The waiter approached with a menu.

"We know what we want," my lover spoke. "Oyster cocktails and Valencia-style paella for both."

She looked at me with her woman's eyes, fathomless and blue like the sea.

꧁~

I don't have much time left. This morning, the sight of an Indian woman breast-feeding her child filled me with a nostalgia for things mammalian. I wrote a long letter to my chil-

dren, but after reading it realized it was full of sentimental
nonsense. I tore it up.

On the third night, we waited till all was quiet before slip-
ping down to the beach. Out at sea, the lanterns of the fishing
boats flickered, the same trawlers that catch my kind with
their treacherous nets. We undressed by the water. She took
me by the arm and led me away from the shore. The cold
didn't affect us, and we floated easily, swept by the tide. Soon
our bellies began to irradiate a reddish-green phosphoresence.
Her abdomen opened to mine, and my pentatentacle sought
its primeval sea warmth. We went under the surface. I was
able to breathe submerged; I was able to breathe through
water as in the beginning of life. I was enveloped by the mother sea and part of me was surrounded by another sea. Suddenly her abdomen shuddered and tightened. Her inside walls
began contracting as if giving birth in reverse. Then her
abdomen closed and severed my tentacle. She fled in a cloud of
ink, abandoning me in the ocean's immensity.

I've just come out of the shower. My skin dries off quickly
if I'm not careful. I must constantly drag myself to the bathroom, attach my suckers to the tile, and let the cool brackish
water run down my body and saturate my thirsty pores. I go
back to bed dripping and cover myself with a wet sheet. I
write these last words with the tip of my right upper tentacle.
I know the end of my human existence is near. Tonight, my
transfigured body will slither through the window and onto
the beach. When the cleaning woman opens the door tomorrow, she'll find my bodily remains. Scattered on the floor nearby, she'll see sheets of a manuscript written in an opaque ink
of unknown origin. The police will look for a pen but will never
find one. They might discover the trail of spittle I'll leave on

the sand as I make my way towards new seas, towards new archipelagos inhabited by voracious females ready to swallow my sterile yet virile pentatentacles. It is possible that if I continue this evolution in reverse, someday I will become an argonaut polypus. In that ideal state my isolation will be absolute, because the hectocotylus of said species has the unique capacity to become detached from the body and gain a life of its own as soon as it reaches reproductive maturity. To be nothing but a phallic being, to know not why nor how, to have but one mission in life with no questions or answers, to enter the womb of an unsuspecting female without the need for excuses, and nothing else.

The Cemetery Facing the Ocean

From Guadalajara to Tepic the road isn't bad. Dangerous, perhaps, but never monotonous. First it goes up over the escarpment and down to a village in a valley where the bus stops for ten minutes and people try to sell the passengers murky mineral water with curative powers from a spring somewhere in the Devil's Backbone. Old ladies reach up to the windows with handfuls of tortillas filled with chile. If you are not nauseated yet from the diesel fuel, you may be tempted to buy a slice of watermelon or papaya or half an avocado that has been sprayed with water endlessly to keep the flies at a distance. Then you make sure you get back on your seat before the driver finishes his business and starts off unannounced. From there on, it's uphill again, all the way to the high plateau.

While she dreams on the soiled headrest, I gaze out the window and see the rows of maguey. They endlessly crisscross until I feel drunk from so much green. The maguey occupies the better land. There are patches of maize clinging precariously to some of the hillsides. I'd like to know how these people convince the earth to give forth enough corn—this dry land strewn with large black boulders that resemble giant obsidian monoliths left behind by the Toltec gods tired of playing children's games.

"It's volcanic soil and volcanic ash is supposed to be very fertile," she explains.

Yes, of course, but I don't see any empirical evidence of volcanic ash. Only boulders. Maybe that's why there are so many quaint stone fences all over the landscape, to move the boulders out of the way.

Then there's a descent, this time a noticeable one. A large, pleasantly green valley extends as far as the eyes can see. At the end of it and to the left there's a small city. I yawn to make my ears pop and be able to hear her description clearly.

"Sugar cane. This is beginning to look like the *tierra caliente*."

Is that so, I say to myself, acknowledging her observation. If she hadn't said anything, I might have believed the cane was extremely tall corn. After all, the leaves of both do look alike.

For some esoteric reason, the bus is on the wrong side of the divided street coming into town. This procedure goes on for about half a kilometer. The oncoming traffic—mostly bicycles and scooters—gracefully veers out of the way. At last the driver turns left into what looks like a brand new bus station. His seemingly peculiar behavior becomes very reasonable when you realize there's a solid concrete island separating the lanes in front of the station.

"I think I better take another Enterovioform after lunch."

Yes. The closer one gets to a tropical environment, the greater the risk of contaminated water and vegetables.

"In fact, we better not drink the water."

Fine. I'd rather drink Dos Equis anyway.

"It always rains in the afternoons in Tepic," someone announced. I was able to understand the friendly *nativo's* Spanish. He spotted the two of us immediately as we stepped off the bus. In Guadalajara, I learned they can identify a gringo by his footwear. The shoeshine boys never leave you alone in the parks and plazas, even if you just had a spit shine. Really, it'd have become a nuisance had it not been for their hungry faces. You can't very well hate a child who's try-

ing to make a living. Next time I'll wear sandals. That ought
to keep those little buzzards away.

Now the rains are making the trip a bit unpleasant. The
bus goes through this town, Compostela, that's full of people
standing under the store awnings watching the downpour. If
it's true that it rains every afternoon, I wonder what effect
this has on a person's mind. Everything looks so distant
through the thick rain, and so hopeless.

"This must be orographic rain."

"Will you explain that, please?"

"The kind that occurs when moist ocean winds run into a
mountain range and are forced upward and the cooler air
above condenses the moisture, resulting in precipitation."

Is there such a thing as pornographic rain?

"Why have you been mumbling all day long?"

Because knowing the cause doesn't change the effects, or
something along those lines.

The bus driver is using a fair amount of common sense,
though. I'm not as apprehensive anymore, seeing he's using
second gear all the way, up and down, up and around these
hills. Mostly down now. The flora is definitely becoming tropical. My ears have been popping continuously and the engine
roars loudly.

A friend of ours said there's this place, a fishing village
that's really rustic. Won't be that way much longer. The *presidente* has big plans for the area, you know, develop it into a
sort of Mexican Riviera. All the way from Maz-at-lhan to
Puerto Vallarta. The government is expropriating the whole
ocean front and moving the people inland. Shit, it's a clean
steal. Anyway, if what you two want is a revitalizing experience, go spend a week there.

"Look, there's the ocean!"

Sure enough. It isn't orographic raining on this side of the mountains. The sea looks calm from up here, perhaps too calm for an ocean. It has no discernable horizon. Calm on the surface but underneath treacherous flows may abound.

He said as soon as you hit the coastal plain to be on the alert. The bus driver won't stop unless you tell him to. They don't give a shit if you end up in Vallarta and have to take a bus back.

After six-and-a-half hours we have safely arrived. I feel quite naked, standing on the highway wearing my silly over-sized American shoes. Everyone's looking at them. That is to say, everyone who happens to be at the small snack-and-refreshment stand where the bus abandoned us. They are drinking coconut milk and inspecting my shoes.

"First thing we're going to do is buy some huaraches," I say.

She has noticed the donkey rummaging through the refuse in the ditch and lets out a cry. It's a three-legged donkey, so to speak. The fourth one is broken at the knee and very much infected. Through the blood and pus a bone can be seen. The flesh twitches periodically, and with every twitch the swarm of flies stirs and settles down again.

A few young boys are vying for the right to carry our suitcase and snorkeling gear. Here's a perfect chance to play God. I must choose one of them. I have three options: select the best specimen and espouse social Darwinism; be a meek Christian and help the underdog; or compromise and tap the in-between. But I am a good God, a magnanimous God. I choose the strongest one to carry the suitcase and the weakest one to tote the skin-diving gear. The third child is left behind, sadly looking down at his swollen stomach and belly button. It's hard to imagine anyone being sad at not having the chance to be a servant.

The street is surprisingly wide, though as yet unpaved. Must be part of the plan to transform all that indigenous but alien beauty into a more acceptable Mediterranean style. In the center they have planted oleanders and palms. Meanwhile the dust clings to my stupid shoes. It hasn't rained on this side of the mountains.

"*¿Cómo te llamas, chico?*"

"Ramiro," he said. He did understand my question. I just said it the way it's written, anyway. How about that.

"*¿Y tu hermano?*"

He's not a brother of mine, he's a cousin. He calls himself something or other because he's so little. Well, I can say it better than understand it. Who knows what the other kid's name is.

The small one kicks Ramiro and begins to run. He runs till there's no more street left, keeps on running on the sand and stops short of jumping into the water. The smell of frying fish touches off a barrage of childhood sensations, from a forgotten family vacation to the Gulf Coast.

"I really feel self-conscious," she says.

"Don't worry about it."

Our friend told us to turn right at the end of the street and you can't help but run into the hotel. It's a two-story building run by an old couple from Los Angeles. That's what they claim. I'm more inclined to believe they are from Haifa. They'll give you a good deal, though.

So we make the right turn and feel relieved at the sight of the Hotel Russell. The baggage boys are afraid to cross the gate, and I give them each a peso for their effort. The object of their fear seems to be a bulging figure dozing off in a rocking chair. What must be his mate gets up to welcome the visitors, and after asking if we are married ("I noticed you don't wear rings") leads us inside a large room full of caged birds and over-ripe fruit. She pulls out a pitcher from an ancient refrigerator.

"I really like your birds," she says.

"I really like this drink," I comment. "What is it?"

"Now, we have rooms with beds for fifty pesos a day, and we also have rooms with cots for thirty pesos. All of the rooms have showers but no hot water."

"Let's take one with cots, that sounds different."

Let's.

"Where can we eat?"

We have discontinued serving meals, she explains, so you have to go out.

Out? Where out?

There's a new restaurant, very nice, very clean, but it's in the next village about three miles down the road.

Check.

"Tonight you'd probably be better off eating at the local place. Just be sure not to eat any uncooked cabbage. Also avoid the lettuce."

Yes, of course.

"We don't run a fancy place like those in Vallarta but nature more than makes up in sheer beauty for what we lack in comfort, don't you agree?"

"Oh definitely," she agrees.

"I'll give you a room upstairs, so you have a better view of the ocean."

That's nice of her.

See Loreta the *guacamaya.*

She was trapped in the perpetual rain forest, her wings were clipped, and now she lives in this tree that blocks the better view of the ocean.

I've already changed into my swimming trunks, but she's still combing her hair and touching up before we go down to the beach.

I notice her nipples harden in front of the mirror like they used to, and I almost go up to her.

The macaw is an extremely colorful bird, even though this one is a female.

"Loreta," I say, and she perks up from her nap. She's inching down a limb toward me. "Loreta," I whisper. She can't resist my call. Not even macaws can ignore my virility.

"Oh, what a beautiful tropical bird!" she shouts.

That ruins it. Loreta's climbing back to her favorite branch. Well, maybe tomorrow.

Who's going to admire her new custom-sewn hot-pink bikini shipped from California? Were I to remark she looks gorgeous, she wouldn't believe me, because I never say such things. Because all compliments are in a way hypocritical.

"You don't seem terribly excited about being here."

Who, me?

"I know what you're thinking; you wish you had gone to Vallarta by yourself and come-what-may."

There's some truth to that, undeniably. But may I ask, what's wrong with come-what-mays?

I go into the room in search of my fins and mask. When I step out she's gone. On my way across the yard I run into a bunch of children, a family that just arrived. A station wagon with Texas plates. Maybe us twelve years hence.

Is it possible? Is it happiness?

I don my mask and sit on the sand next to her, hissing through the snorkel.

"Shit," she snaps sharply.

A couple of local beach boys pass by displaying their sun-blackened muscles. Their heads rotate so as to keep their eyes on her thighs.

"They're dying to screw you, baby."

"Goddammit, fuck you," she bursts out in a strange tone.

That's the first time ever she's said those words to me. She gets up and dashes for the water, maybe to wash away some tears. Wash away, wash away. I almost warn her about the undertow. I know I'm being a bastard, that some perverse spirit has polluted my feelings, and yet I can't stop.

"Hey, watch out for the undertow!"

I imagine her being dragged away, and I see myself jumping in to save her life, but too late. Her body appears some hours later face down on the sand, her black hair contrasting more than ever with the pale bloodless skin.

Those are evil thoughts.

I'm rescued by Ramiro and his two friends. They're more interested in the fins than in me, I'm certain.

I think he has asked where we're from. I feel proud of my two years of college Spanish. Of course he doesn't recognize where we're from, so I say it's two-thousand miles to the north. He still has a puzzled look on his face so I explain as best I can it takes fifty hours of continuous travel by bus. That confuses him all the more, judging by his silence. Now I'm not so sure if it is because he doesn't understand my Spanish—A basic course, Audio-Lingual Method—or whether he can't comprehend time and space in those terms.

"*¿Cuántos años tienes?*"

"*Catorce.*"

He's fourteen. Then it's true that the wealthy get bigger and the poor smaller. Their brains supposedly shrink, too.

There come the two beach boys again.

She claims not to be interested in any other man whatsoever. I suppose that should be flattering, but it's hard to believe.

"*¿Estudias?*" Now, I'm getting more daring wanting to know if he goes to school.

"*No, trabajo en el campo con mi padre.*" So he works on the farm with his father. I got that.

I invite him to try on the mask. It's too large for him, so I adjust the straps. There's no way to adjust the fins so he'll have to do without them. I pick up a smooth stone, make it skim over the surf, and challenge him by sign language to find it.

My skin's getting hot, so I go in for a dip and to show off my powerful butterfly stroke to the beach boys who are walking very slowly and glancing at her. However, the salt water proves to be too much for my unprotected eyes and I have to quit after four or five strokes.

I dog-paddle up to her, in a conciliatory mood.

Remember the time we made love in a Florida beach right in front of everyone? I take hold of her waist underwater, my thumbs meeting on her navel, my palms spreading over her hips.

Ramiro, you little son of a gun. You're supposed to be looking for the stone and instead you turn out to be a submarine voyeur. Interesting how the sexual apparatus doesn't seem to suffer from malnutrition the way brains allegedly do. Well, what can you expect. I used to do the same when I was his age. And when I was older, too, for that matter. Much older.

The sea is exerting its powers. I feel strangely invigorated yet relaxed. My appetite is awakening as is my thirst. I've taken note of a little bar up the beach a ways. I ask her to go with me and she accepts. She's in a fairly good mood. Amazing how far a little caress will go. Why don't I show her more affection? It ought to be so easy, so simple. It'd be so effortless to manipulate her emotions, to let her dream. For example:

"Someday I'd like to adopt a Mexican or Brazilian child."

Her eyes truly sparkle at the idea.

"Why one or the other, why not both?" she dreams.

"Yes, but not till we have a couple of our own."

She wants to know when she can stop taking the pill. I tell her if I were her I'd stop without letting me know and surprise me with the good news.

I'm stunned by the absurdity of such a conversation in this setting, and by my continuing cruelty.

We dry each other off and walk toward the bar, holding hands. Ramiro and his friends start to follow us, but I tell them to keep on playing with the snorkel. It takes quite an effort to structure a sentence to convey that command. I should have used the subjunctive, I now realize. Somehow the instructor's explanation that the subjunctive is the mood of unreality and uncertainty makes more sense than ever.

The bar is authentically rustic. I comment to her that it is funny how affluent societies try to imitate poverty in certain buildings.

"I never thought of it that way," she says. I feel proud of my observation.

I order a coke for her and a beer for me. The few fishermen can't help but look at her. It doesn't strike me as an obscene stare like the beach boys', but rather one of curiosity. I'm careful not to alienate them with my own curiosity. They all have eroded faces, like the slopes we crossed. If they only knew how hard they work so that we may play.

There's a small basket on the counter full of tomatoes. I ask the proprietor for one and he deftly cuts it in six even slices. She reminds me of the lady's warning, but I am confident that I possess a stronger-than-average gastro-intestinal system. I never got sick when I was in Europe.

"You're going to have trouble pooping if you don't eat any fruit," I say, offering a slice, knowing she'll refuse it.

"That's okay. I know I can handle constipation, but I'm not sure about amoebic dysentery."

The tomatoes are unbelievably tasty. Could it possibly be due to the use of human fertilizer? I can just see the cycle. You eat produce fertilized with your excrement so you can have more excrement to fertilize your vegetables. I voice this brilliant discovery to her and she becomes offended, almost nauseated. How can you eat after that, she wonders. In the meantime the nine-percent alcohol by volume has begun to permeate my whole being. A few more bottles and I will not give a damn about much, not even myself.

There's a picturesque scene unfolding on the shore a couple of hundred yards away. A once-in-a-lifetime opportunity for us tourists. A small rowboat is dropping a net in a semicircle. Someone is holding one end standing on the beach while his partners close the trap. We rush to the scene. I, clutching a fresh bottle of cerveza. By the time we arrive, they are pulling the net from both ends. A few children are inside the loop splashing water, obviously trying to scare the fish so they get entangled in the net. Only the smart ones survive a bit longer by jumping over.

"There's a good metaphor of marriage," I say.

"What do you mean?" she asks.

"The tightening semicircle," I answer. "The attempt to escape the trap, but without realizing it you're swimming deeper into the funnel."

She turns and walks away from me. I've done it again.

The catch is quite varied. I'm ignorant of the nomenclature of most of the species. Some apparently aren't esteemed as food and are thrown back into the water. Shocked by the experience, they cannot swim at first. A few, I notice, aren't able to swim again. They just drift on the surface, drifting dead, rocked gently by the waves.

The center of attention is a turtle of moderate size. I'm no expert, but it seems to me that it's an unusual catch. The children have turned it over on its back and are poking sticks into its anus.

"What are they doing?" she exclaims in disbelief.

"Nothing. What we have here is a mild case of latent homosexuality," I lecture in a nasal tone. Something within me is revolted by the statement.

"Goddammit, I'm sick of your sarcasm. Do something about it. Please!"

What can I do about it? I have enough common sense not to interfere with children in front of their parents, especially in a foreign culture. I don't know how the fathers might react.

She tries to do something about it. She approaches one of the kids and jerks the stick out of his hand. It was an unexpected move and the rest of the children are intimidated.

"Help me turn him over."

I'm about to do that, ashamed perhaps at my lack of valor. But one of the fishermen gestures menacingly to leave it alone. For a change I honestly try to be tender with her, leading her away from the crowd as she sobs convulsively.

She asks repeatedly why it has to be like that. I can't think of an answer that would soothe her. I say something about cultural conditioning, that we are suffering from a small dosage of cultural shock.

We are swept away from the village towards the setting sun like pieces of driftwood. This will be the first time either of us witnesses a sunset over the Pacific. We've seen a few over the Gulf of Mexico, secure ones—land always but a skip and jump beyond the horizon. But this is not a mere gulf we are facing; it is a fathomless chasm the immensity of which intimidates and overwhelms. All is silent now, we are all alone; the last thatched hut lies a good quarter mile behind, yet we keep on walking westward in a last-ditch attempt to postpone the inevitable. Then we see the clearing. We are attracted to it by the golden reflections emanating from an array of stones. We think it might be a pre-Colombian ruin, but instead we find the village cemetery. The tombstones all face the sunset.

We have arrived at our destination.

—⚭

"My asshole is burning," I say. "This cheap tissue is worse than sandpaper."

"You can use some of my Kleenex," she says. "How many times have you gone?"

"At least four," I say.

"You shouldn't have eaten the tomato," she says. "You're lucky we have a decent toilet in this place."

"Do you think you caught cold last night?"

"Think so. That was some rain."

"Will you be ready soon?" I ask after an awkward pause.

"Another twenty minutes or so," she answers.

"I'll go pay the bill."

Outside I say good morning to Loreta. Her feathers seem much brighter after the downpour. She's having a mango for breakfast. This time she pays no attention to me whatsoever.

I can see and hear the family from Texas having whole-some fun on the beach.

Mrs. Russell's wearing the dress she wore yesterday. She invites me into the living room. I hear her husband coughing in the bathroom, and then the toilet being flushed. She's surprised we're leaving after only one night. I reassure her that we're quite happy with the arrangements, but that my wife came down with dysentery and that I'd like to get her to a doctor in Vallarta. She commends me for being so considerate. In turn I thank her for fixing us soup and sandwiches last night. She assures me that my wife must have developed the diarrhea from our lunch in Tepic. I beg her to forgive me, that I wasn't trying to imply something was wrong with her food. I give her a twenty-dollar bill and insist she keep the change.

I return to our room. I was hoping to catch her crying, but she has managed to regain her composure.

"Almost ready," she says. "There's your bag. I wasn't able to fit much into it, but it'll be enough to get you home. I put a few Kleenex right on top just in case."

"Thanks," I say.

"I hope we don't have a long wait for a bus," she says at last.

"We won't," I say. "Mrs. Russell told me there's one going in either direction every half-hour."

The Forbidden Fruit
Was a Papaya

I shall have confessed my sins but to three men of the
cloth when my life comes to its foregone conclusion: Father
Federico, Father Carbonell, and Father Rae, the fiery vicar
who heard my first confession in America, which turned out to
be my last ever. In all fairness, the Irish imbecile is not entirely at fault for this turn of events, for my faith had been criti-
cally crippled years before when the Virgin failed to save my
mutt, which had been poisoned along with thirty-two other
male dogs in the infamous Varadero canine massacre of 1954.
But he must bear partial responsibility for the potential loss
of a soul, though Mother blames Fidel Castro alone for derail-
ing world history as well as my spiritual fate. That pivotal
confession, given in broken English at a church in Coral
Gables in the summer of 1960, should have been heard in
Spanish by Father Carbonell at the chapel of Santa Teresita
de Jesús sometime after September, 1959, for the purported
mortal sin that provoked Rae's wrath was committed on
Cuban soil (sand, to be exact, because the event happened on
the beach) with the help of a Cuban girl.

Even though the traumatic experience with Father Rae
drove me from the confessional forever, my earliest memories
of the cathartic ritual are splashed with the sweet scents of
talcum powder and eau de lilac that emanated from the ethe-
real Father Federico, who embodied the concept of the Holy
Ghost I had fashioned in my childish imagination. Confession
with him amounted to little more than a soliloquy, for he was
in his eighties and almost deaf when I took my First Communion. Before puberty I committed no sins of consequence. I

was a mama's boy, used no foul language, obeyed authority, told the truth most of the time, yet I was forced to confess regularly and admit to transgressions simply because it was possible I might have indulged in their contemplation. Later, as I reached puberty, I started sinning "in thought." For instance, the most common Cuban slang term for the female genital is "papaya." I spent many hours trying to imagine how this fruit might appear dangling between a woman's legs. Maybe the womb looked like the inside of one; that would explain why the prayer said "Blessed is the fruit of thy womb, Jesus." At any rate, a whole fruit didn't make much sense. It wasn't until I saw the possibility of a *slice* of papaya that the image coalesced, and when the taste and aroma of this tropical delight were added, the fantasy of seeing a woman's papaya became an obsession, though I didn't know what to make of all the seeds papayas have. But, either Father Federico was too senile to understand my allusions or my fantasy was common to the collective psyche of pubescent Cubans, for he didn't increase the penance from his usual three Hail Marys and a Credo when I described it to him.

From my perspective, there were other advantages to having Federico as our priest. Mass during his tenure was strictly a thirty-minute affair. To begin with, he never gave sermons, reading instead the gospel for the day in the vernacular. He had trained Pepe, the altar boy—who was really a man in his thirties—to be lightning quick with his responses, so much so that one had the impression celebrant and acolyte were racing each other. Unconsciously, the congregation did its best to keep up with the frenzied pace, genuflecting, making the sign of the cross, standing and sitting so swiftly that the ritual lost all semblance of holiness. Communion lasted but a couple of minutes, for only the most pious ladies took part in it. Father Federico had foregone public collections so

as not to embarrass the congregation, which was largely poor.
By the time the old pastor dismissed Mass with the command,
"Ite, Missa Est," the small nave was deserted. He himself
taught that the obligation to the Third Commandment was
fulfilled if one stayed through the Eucharist.

But the primary reason I'll always remember Father Federico with fondness is the emphasis he placed on the cult of
the Virgin. I do not know how widespread this practice is
throughout the Catholic world; for all I know, he invented it.
Each evening during May, Pepe would start ringing the bells
at seven, in five-minute intervals, announcing the service that
began at seven-thirty. People who never set foot in church the
rest of the year swarmed to the temple to sing hymns in
praise of Mary. There was one requirement for admission:
Everyone had to bring an offering of freshly-cut flowers. In
April the rains returned, and in May, flowers were in full
bloom. Bouquets of bougainvillea, oleander, bell flowers and
jasmine were laid in bountiful heaps across the altar, infusing
the temple with an intoxicating, almost aphrodisiacal fra-
grance more pagan than holy. There was no mention of death
or damnation in the psalms led by Father Federico, only the
promise of life eternal and heavenly bliss. It was during one of
these mystical celebrations that, after my arm accidentally
pressed against the blossoming breast of María Machado, I
experienced my first involuntary erection.

Church was never the same after Father Federico passed
away. His replacement, a strict, sour, anachronistic peninsu-
lar bigot named Carbonell, believed humans to be inherently
evil, particularly when subjected to the erotic influences of
tropical climates. Thus, one of the most radical changes he
made was to abolish Federico's Flowers of May cult, decreeing
it deviated dangerously from the orthodox teachings of Rome.
He also tried, without much success, to prevent the town from

partaking in carnival, claiming that the African rhythms of the congas were driven by demonic forces. As an alternative to those paganistic celebrations, he offered a morbid program for Lent, complete with a recreation of the Passion through the previously placid streets of Varadero. Since he was Spanish, short, plump, and red-faced, someone quickly dubbed him "the Fig," and the nickname caught on. We could hardly understand his thick Castillian accent at first, and to make matters worse, he spoke as if his mouth were full of mashed potatoes.

Masses became excruciating marathons. To prevent tardiness and the early exodus of the congregation, Father Carbonell barred the doors before the service began. Once safely corralled, the flock was subjected to theatric performances highlighted by bombastic sermons. Even Pepe was transformed. After a few months of tutoring by the Fig, he was articulating his responses in clear, impeccable Latin.

Father Carbonell had a table worked out which showed exactly how many years in Purgatory every kind of sin earned, and he posted it on the door to remind passersby of the consequences of sinning. Eternity was forever, so a hundred years for missing mass was a mere tick of the eternal clock. A minor profanity such as "damn" earned the culprit twenty years. The wickedness of going to a whorehouse was incalculable; he couldn't begin to estimate how many millennia it'd take to atone for such a sin. However, in his opinion, the worst transgression was homosexuality, an offense so perverse that it rendered salvation nearly impossible.

Needless to say, I dreaded going to confession with Father Carbonell. I postponed the tête-à-tête as long as I could, pretending to be ill or too busy with schoolwork, or arguing that I had committed no mortal sins. But Mother explained that an accumulation of peccadillos could add up to a mortal sin, so one Saturday she ordered the maid to escort me to church and make sure I entered the confessional.

I was shaking when I knelt down. I was so upset that I traced the sign of the cross in reverse order. The odor of garlic hit my nostrils like a fist. At that moment, I wished Father Federico would somehow resurrect and fill the confessional with his soothing fragrances, for it was obvious Father Carbonell hadn't learned to disguise his rancid secretions in the tropical heat. I stammered badly through the "Forgive me, Father, for I have sinned," and he immediately ordered me to speak loudly and clearly. I had rehearsed my confession well, so I was able to reel off six-months' worth of half-lies, questionable behavior, bad words, and naughty thoughts in one breath. Relieved I had unloaded my sins so easily, I bowed humbly to accept my sentence.

"You call that a confession?" he remarked icily.

"Father Federico…"

"Father Federico, Father Federico, bless his soul, but obviously he didn't know how to take confessions. How old are you?"

"Twelve."

"You can't be so innocent at your age. You'll have to be more specific with me. How many lies? To whom? Were they mere fibs or calumnies? What bad words? What nasty thoughts? Give me examples. Illustrate."

I was caught completely off guard. My mind was in turmoil, frantically switching from bad word to bad word, trying to select one that wouldn't elicit his anger. I didn't dare say "shit," much less "I shit on the Lord." I discarded the Spanish equivalents of crap, asshole, fuck, and several of its variants. The most abused Cuban obscenity is *coño*; it is uttered by men and women alike for any or no reason at all, to open and close exclamations, to show anger or pleasure, approval or disapproval, agreement or disbelief. I thought I'd be safe admitting to its use.

"I have said *coño* at least a hundred times, Father."

I had no idea *coño* was the Castillian equivalent of *papaya*. Carbonell exploded so violently that he showered my face with garlic saliva.

"Have you no shame whatsoever? Do you know what you're saying? Jesús, María y José!"

It took me a good forty-five minutes to repeat a Credo/ Pater Noster/Hail Mary combination by each Station of the Cross. I left in tears. My eyes were so bloodshot that when I got home Mother asked what was wrong. I was afraid to tell the truth, so I covered up by saying I fell down and hurt my knees, which were raw from the prolonged penance. This lie earned me three rosaries the next time I went to confession.

⊘∭~

Mother was ecstatic with the new priest. Father Federico may have been a kind old man, bless his soul, but as spiritual leader he left much to be desired. At last we had a true theologian, a moralist who'd show the town the road to salvation. As a consequence, doctrine was crammed down my throat at every opportunity. I even had to start memorizing the Latin responses to Mass, which could only mean I was being groomed as a back-up to Pepe. Fortunately, my father's machismo put an end to Mother's designs. His only son, he declared unequivocally, would not wear girlish gowns. He did allow me to dress up as a shepherd in Carbonell's first Christmas program. María Machado played the Virgin, a role that suited her perfectly since she inherited her Lebanese mother's emerald eyes and olive skin. I was trembling as I approached the altar with my offering of incense. As I knelt down to kiss the porcelain Baby Jesus cradled in her arms, I stumbled and buried my face in her excited chest.

The uproar of the congregation still rings in my ears, but the embarrassment I suffered was a small price to pay to be in Heaven for five seconds. From that point on, I was consumed by the remembrance of the contact with María's breasts. I believed I was in love. I started going for long walks along the beach until sundown, to compose poems in her honor. I ignored my friends, neglected my studies, became hypnotized by the sea. When I woke up several months later, my body had undergone changes as pronounced as those taking place in the political arena of Cuba.

My friends welcomed me back to the circle. They too had gone through different stages of a metamorphosis. Before, the main topic of our bull sessions had been baseball. Now we wanted to discuss girls. One night Aldo brought a paperback he'd swiped from an older brother to our meeting place behind José's bar. The story, I will never forget, was titled "The Pleasures of Lesbia." Aldo explained that Lesbia was not a woman's name, as we thought offhand, but rather the scientific term for women who did dirty things to one another. Sure enough, the pages of the book, which proclaimed proudly to have been "Made in Mexico," was generously illustrated with grainy, sepia-toned photographs of women engaged in a variety of acts. I was so far behind my age group in sexual education that this marked the first time I had seen a true representation of adult female genitalia. I brought up the fact that there was absolutely no resemblance, at least visually, between the fruit we called a papaya and the papayas of these women. Was it because they were "lesbian?" We argued this seeming contradiction heatedly until Guaco, who always was a step ahead of the gang, came up with the idea that you'd have to taste one to make a final judgment.

The inevitable followed. I was thirteen. I was achieving gratuitous erections at the most unexpected times and least acceptable places. I didn't have an older brother to teach me the facts of life. I could only go by what the paperbacks from Mexico and the other boys said. The word *masturbation* was not in our vocabulary. A translation of the phrase commonly used to describe the act would be to "pump one's well." Guaco claimed that if you pumped your well very fast, you'd eventually make it "come." It took some doing, but I finally succeeded. I handled my penis so vigorously, though, that the experience was more painful than pleasurable. As soon as I finished, I regretted it immensely, for I knew I'd have to confess to the Fig.

I rehearsed for the confession as if my life depended on it. I didn't know for sure what sort of sin this was, but I was certain it fell in the disgusting category. Mother had done an excellent job of making me feel guilty about any physiological function which involved an emission. Defecation, urination, the passing of gas, belching—these were shameful manifestations of the animalistic in our bodies. Repulsive as they might be, they could not be considered sinful, but this new perturbing experience had to be worth at least a thousand years of banishment from Paradise. There was in our Holy Scriptures text a depiction of souls expiating in Purgatory, anguished naked humanoids *sans* genitals trapped in hideous landscapes, flames spewing all about. The very absence of genitals suggested very strongly that *these* had been responsible for the souls' downfall. I feared Carbonell, to be sure, but not nearly as much as this vision concocted by some demented Spanish baroque artist.

I knelt down. Inside the confessional, Father Carbonell was fanning his obese body. Each stroke propelled a ripple of garlic breath through the screen. I rushed through the opening prayer hoping to set a quick tempo to the ordeal, but he ordered me to slow down and pronounce clearly.

I soon exhausted my repertoire of minor offenses. I confessed to several I hadn't even committed recently just to postpone the moment of reckoning. My ears were hot; my knees wobbled under the pressure. I opened my mouth but no words came out.

"What else?" the Fig demanded impatiently. "I haven't got all day."

I was cornered. Try as I might, the words refused to come out. It was simply too humiliating, even if God in his omniscience knew I was withholding information. I decided instead to tell about the Mexican books.

"I saw pictures of women in a magazine."

"What sort of pictures?" he retorted in his inquisitor's tone.

"Naked women. They were kissing each other's papayas," I whispered.

Carbonell cleared his throat. There was a terrifying pause during which his heavy, belabored breathing and my heartbeat raced to a dead heat.

"I assume," he said in a very low voice though no one was within earshot, "you mean to say they were kissing each other's breasts."

"No, Father. They were kissing each other's *coños*," I clarified hoarsely.

"Holy Mother of God!" Carbonell exhaled.

"Who conceived without sin," I responded like a well-trained acolyte.

I fled in panic when he finished his tirade. In punishment, he forbid me to taste my favorite dessert for three months, which at the time happened to be guava paste with cream cheese. It was then I developed an insatiable craving for papaya halves in heavy syrup.

⊙∰∽

I would have to wait several years to settle once and for all the question of the papaya, to experience for myself the unexpected sensorial correspondences between the actual and the metaphoric fruit, but I didn't have to wait so long for the confession that resulted in my self-imposed excommunion from Rome.

The eve of our humiliating departure from Cuba to the jeers of the proletariat, I mustered enough courage to declare my everlasting love to María. Her sister, who was chaperoning our walk, let us slip to the beach for our farewell. It was the first time ever we had been alone. I was trembling quite uncontrollably as we hurried to the wooden pier that was erected every summer to moor the glass-bottomed boat. We stopped at the water's edge next to the ramp leading up to the pier. The sea was calm. In the moonless sky, the Milky Way pointed towards a new life to the north. Inspired by the anguish of an uncertain future, I recited one of the poems I had composed in her honor the year before. Choking with emotion, I made the promise that someday, somehow, I'd return to marry her. María was so moved that in the ensuing embrace, she took my inexperienced, frightened hand on a tortuous journey over her body, finally placing it over her sex. It felt as if I were touching a breathing coral, not a papaya, and I withdrew my hand with a jerk, afraid it'd burn if I left it on her for even one second. Then she held my erection in her hand and the moonless sky exploded in a rain of shooting stars.

-⚉✿©

Approximately one year later, Mother declared my English fluent enough to attempt a confession. After recreating the scene with María a thousand times during that first sad year of exile, I had come to realize there was nothing sinful about what we had done. But to please my mother I entered Father Rae's confessional one fine Saturday afternoon. But Mother had incorrectly gauged my fluency in our adopted language. I mistakenly confessed María and I had "made love." Father Rae's reaction was much more violent than any of Carbonell's. He was so angry I thought he'd come out of the confessional to choke me. He terrorized me with a rambling, vitriolic lecture about sex much beyond my level of proficiency at the time. At long last he asked that I show repentance by reciting the Act of Contrition. Before agreeing to go to confession, I had told Mother I wasn't ready yet to recite this important prayer in English. But she assured me it was quite permissible to say any prayer in any language, since God was omniscient. She had judged wrong once again.

"You don't even know the Act of Contrition!" Father Rae interrupted in disbelief before I reached the halfway point. "What garbage are you saying?"

"Excuse me, Father. I am Cuban, so I am praying it in Spanish," I explained.

Father Rae showed no mercy. His reply came in a tone, timbre, and pitch I had no problem interpreting:

"Go to Hell, you little Cuban fornicator!"

But not to worry. Father Rae's damnation notwithstanding, if there's such a thing as Glory as described by the Catholic Church, I am assured salvation by a papal bull purchased by my family which guarantees our decadent line the chance to repent at the last possible instant, even if we take our own lives. When we fled our homeland on that distant day in 1959, one of the few items Mother salvaged from the airport search was the frame enclosing the ironclad certificate. The militiamen simply laughed at the beatific image of Pope Pius the Something holding up two delicate fingers in an ineffectual gesture. On the other hand, they turned deadly serious when her silver and gold rosary, which she was trying to smuggle out, dropped from her eyeglasses case. It was nationalized on the spot in the name of the Revolution, to help buy guns to protect the Fatherland from the reactionary forces of imperialism, of which religion was a powerful ally.

The Zib and the Masseur

The oldest of men tell the tale of the rise of a dormant zib and the subsequent downfall of a great masseur, whose delicate yet potent hands succeeded in kneading out every pain and calamity that ailed the noble and corrupt flesh of his wealthy clients. Kings, sheiks, emirs, and viziers from all the known territories of this earthly and fleeting kingdom of Allah made the pilgrimage to his steaming baths in order to experience the miracle of his heavenly hands, assured by those who had been healed by their magic that they would be rewarded with a foretaste of divine bliss.

The story goes that the only son of a very powerful and venerated emir had apparently been cursed with the most horrible, pitiful misfortune that can befall a man, and that the father, having himself experienced the wondrous qualities of the masseur's hands on numerous occasions, sent his progeny to the fabled baths in hopes that the magician of the flesh would make his instrument of pleasure respond to stimulus as expected. This young lad was otherwise blessed with the most sensuous body ever seen by mortal eyes. What abundance of forms! What soft, milk-white skin! Indeed, Nature had spun pillows of silken flesh at the most delectable and strategic places.

When the masseur saw this lovely body sleeping on the marble table, his soul attempted to escape from its prison and rush to embrace that example of carnal perfection. For, although married to a diligent wife who at that very moment was home nursing their third child, the good masseur traveled the anal road in both directions. Taking advantage of the fact his presence hadn't been noticed, the man permitted his eyes to feast on the naked body. The youth turned slightly as if pricked by the intensity of the voyeur's inspection, assuming a provocative position that excited the masseur's imagination all the more. Slowly, anxious to prolong the precious encounter, the masseur approached the table and began to massage the boy's back, savoring every inch of flesh until his fingers reached the region where the body forks into two rivers of lust. But what a terrifying discovery he made when he finally turned the slumbering youth over! The oldest of men claim that the masseur let out an anguished cry that was heard beyond the fortified walls of the city when he saw that the lad's zib was not larger than a hazelnut. His lusty dreams quickly turned to tears, evaporating like the steam rising from the floor. The boy, who was by now awake and well aware of the reason for the masseur's unhappiness, joined him with a heartbreaking sob.

"Oh, what great evil deeds your father must have committed to provoke the wrath of Allah," the masseur wailed. "Surely this is in punishment so you won't spread his wicked seed. But the father should be the one punished, not the innocent offspring. What will life be for you without a zib and its delicious consequences?"

The boy cried louder, like a goat that is to be sacrificed, convinced that it'd be better to die than to go through manhood not equipped with an adequate tool. At last he managed to tell the masseur that his father had offered a saddlebag full of gold as a just reward to the person who succeeded in bringing his zib to life.

Far more interested in the potential erotic rewards if he were able to awaken the hibernating asp, the masseur invoked all of his expertise and set out to exorcise the inertia that made the boy's zib limp and pathetically small. Never before, say the old men who kept this story alive through the river of time, had his extraordinary hands worked with such rhythmic precision and eloquence. Yet the masterfully stimulated zib did not grow beyond the size of a normal walnut.

But wise men teach us never to lose all hope, for the intentions of Allah are seldom clearly revealed to mortal men. At this point, when all seemed destined to failure, the boy timidly suggested that perhaps the presence of a woman might help turn the unfavorable tide of events around.

"Master," he told the masseur with shyness, "if my honorable father's carnal inheritance is so small, it is not his fault. I am to blame for not having tried to make it prosper. For how do you expect a kid to become a powerful he-goat if it avoids the willing she-goats? How can a seedling grow to be a tree without being irrigated?"

"Or how can a shepherd lean on his staff when it isn't any longer than a bone from his little finger?" mused the masseur.

"Go find me a suitable woman with whom I can start my exercises," suggested the boy. "I will divide the gold my father gave me between you regardless of the outcome."

The masseur promptly obeyed, leaving the premises engrossed in these thoughts: "That naive lad believes that a zib is like soft candy paste, which spreads out the more you work it! How can anyone think that a blossom becomes a cucumber overnight, or that a plantain fills its skin with pulp by simply blowing air into it?"

Resigned to the fact that this magnificent virgin body was not to be one with his, and convinced that the boy presented no danger to his honor as a husband, the man went to fetch his wife with the intention of keeping all the gold in the family.

Once he reached home he told her, "Oh, mother of Ali! I have just massaged a boy as beautiful as a full desert moon, the son of a great emir, whose body is blessed with heavenly perfection. But the poor lad is miserably endowed with a zib not larger than a hazelnut! He thinks that contact with a woman will make it erect, and since he's dividing the reward between the woman who does him the favor and me, I thought we could keep it all in the family. He need not know you are my wife. So leave the infant sleeping, and let's go quickly. It won't take more than an hour."

Listen to me, wretched men who toil in this ephemeral life! Never trust your wife with another man, not even if that man be your own brother, not even if that man be an eunuch, for a woman has no control over her passions! This is what happened.

As soon as the ignorant masseur left his wife in the steam chamber where the boy was waiting for his go-between to provide a remedy for his illness, as soon as she caught a glimpse of the seemingly impotent emir's son, her flesh flushed, her nipples quivered under the robe and her womanly fluids rushed to make the gate passable to a soldier's lance. She bolted the door from within as her husband had stupidly instructed her to do and began to undress immediately, savoring visually the splendorous virginal figure lying on the marble surface. For a moment, but only for a second, a dark cloud of disappointment glazed her ebony eyes as she noticed the minute zib hidden away in the folds of his thighs. For if the boy was the synthesis of male beauty, this woman was his image mirrored in the antiethical sex, and like two opposite poles obeying the immutable laws of magnetism, they attracted each other violently, sending off charged particles that caused the slumbering zib to stand up vigorously and become engorged till it was as large as a good cucumber grown in the floodplains of the Nile.

What more can be said except that the inevitable
occurred? She rushed to his side and fondled the throbbing zib
in her expert hands, gauging the force of the stream of blood
that had finally shattered the accursed dam. The neophyte
moaned in exquisite pain as her avid tongue made the voyage
around the penile peninsula, while her fingers shamelessly
assaulted the testicular mounds and pulled teasingly on the
sparsely populated pubic forest. Unable to prolong the agony
of expectation very long, she mounted the stag and rode it
gently at first, allowing the boundaries of the flesh to melt
before embarking on the ritual that draws forth the fluid carrying the mystery of life.

The emir's son proved to be an uncanny pupil. In his first
lesson, he was exposed to and learned intricate secrets that
take a normal man five years to master after his first copulation. Until that day, his had been an untapped well of virility.
It was written that the masseur's wife should discover this
eternal font of pleasure to replenish her unbridled eroticism.

All the while, the masseur watched in astonishment from
a concealed vantage point as his wife inflicted double injury
upon him—being adulterous and depriving him of a lover. In
his despair he cried out to her, "Woman, it is the hour for you
to go home and nurse our infant son. You musn't neglect your
motherly duties." To this she replied in the frenzy of a fifth
encounter within two hours' time, "From this day till I die I
shall not give my breast to another babe other than this one.
He may nibble all he wants and never hear me say 'that's
enough.'"

Thus our true story has come to its conclusion. It was self-
evident to the sorrowful masseur as it is surely transparent to
those of you who are listening that Fate would not be contra-
dicted. Grief-stricken but resigned to the inscrutable designs
of Heaven, the poor man sought the highest minaret in the

city and, after praying for his abandoned children, threw his body to the alley below.

Remember this tale for the rest of your worldly existence, you poor pawns of destiny! A man may believe he can build a perfect triangle to sustain his temporal happiness, but this structure will collapse unless all its sides are kept equidistant.

Exposures

A blast rattled the foundations last night, and afterwards gunfire cracked sporadically for hours. I slept as in a shallow grave, dreaming my eyes had been gouged, and that in their place, black metallic shutters sprang incessantly to reveal gruesome slices of reality. I awoke to the crash of a brief, hard rain, and I am scanning the streets for signs of the struggle when construction crews report to work at the site below. The sky has cleared and the light of the impending sunrise reflecting off the snow-capped volcano is dazzling, but I use the zoom to observe the unsuspecting workers instead. I can almost feel the warmth of the fire they fuel, can almost touch a young boy's face as he awaits his ration of tortillas and beans. For a fleeting moment, I am at his side staring at the decaying walls he and his companions must tear down, the piles of rubble they must remove all day long, but the foreman's whistle shatters the spell and I retreat to the dark room.

It is apparent they have arranged for my accommodations in one of the better hotels of the city. I was surprised to find wall-to-wall carpeting in a semi-tropical climate and a television set in the room. The tiled bathroom has a separate spigot for drinking water, and there's an ample supply of hot water for bathing. When I turn on the shower, a cloud of steam quickly fogs the mirror. I stay under the stream until my muscles relax, all the while making a rough plan of what I must do. Before getting dressed I lay my equipment out on the bed and proceed to clean it meticulously as a hired killer might, anxious to start my job.

⊘∬∫∼

My job is to photograph, not to write. To promote, not document. To shoot the perfect exposure, not to expose. For this I have come armed with three-hundred rounds of assorted film and a bag full of tricks. I can use a UV15 or a Haze 2A to manipulate ultra-violet and heighten dull colors. Or a Sky 1A to reduce blue and add warmth to scenes. Or an 85N6 which, combined with ND 0.4, allows larger apertures to decrease depth of field and blur undesirable backgrounds. When I return, the experts at the agency will choose maybe ten, at most twelve slides to submit to the Tourism Ministry for approval. They have given me a list of places to cover and subjects to cover up. Someone else has already written the brochure. I was hired to fill frames with shapes and colors seductive to the eye. My job is to choose the optimum film, the appropriate lens, the correct aperture and speed. To polarize light and create illusions of bluer skies, to screen out the smog, to show freshly painted façades, to deceive.

⊘∬∫∼

I turn on the television hoping to catch reports of the night's events. Only two stations are broadcasting. The first one is running a Three Stooges episode; the film is badly damaged and the superimposed language doesn't synchronize with the movement of lips on the screen, a flaw that enhances the slapstick to a level of absurdity. I switch channels and for a few minutes drift to another time as I recognize a cartoon I must have watched twenty years ago, as far removed from reality as the dubbed voices are from the animated characters.

At breakfast I ask the waiter about the explosion and gunfire. He doesn't like to discuss politics, he explains, but he heard the bomb was planted by terrorists in a car belonging to a police captain. The gunfire came from an ambush of an army patrol, but the soldiers escaped and gave chase on foot, killing three guerrillas.

I study the map of the city given to the agency by the tourism office. The map suggests a chaotic growth, with far more diagonal intersections than right-angle crossings. A spiral can be discerned, bursting out like shrapnel. Circled in red are the sections of the city I am to shoot, with the main plaza as the focal point.

I read from the text of the brochure:

> When the Conquistadores marched into our capital in the early Sixteenth Century, they discovered a splendor far brighter than any they had seen in the Old World. The chroniclers described to their king and queen temples whose walls were of solid gold, countless marketplaces where all sorts of goods exchanged hands, botanical and zoological gardens, magnificent palaces, even restaurants and hotels. The same fascination holds true for the modern visitor. This advanced yet ancient city has everything one would expect a great metropolis to offer, usually at far lower rates than its counterparts around the world.

Outside the hotel a group of taxi drivers and tour guides interrupt their chatter when they see me coming down the steps. There aren't many tourists staying here, a fact that makes the competition fierce. They push and shove as they try to outbid one another for my patronage. One driver shouts he'll take me to the pyramids for fifteen dollars; a second one quickly undercuts him by offering to do the same for ten. I decline, choosing to walk instead in the direction of the Plaza Mayor.

The city is bustling with activity, undeterred by the evening's violence. Fruit vendors, lottery peddlers, newspaper barkers line the sidewalks and riddle pedestrians with frenzied calls, as if their very existence depended on a missed sale. Indian merchants display handcrafted goods on tattered mats. The smell of secret spices fills the air. Children sleep next to charcoal burners or build pyramids with dried peppers. At a corner an old man plays a haunting melody on a flute. He plays the lament tirelessly, pausing only seconds to say thank you when someone drops a coin in the receptacle by his feet. I move closer looking for a better angle. I am deeply disturbed when I see he has thick membranes covering the cavities where his eyes should be. The sight is repulsive, but some force compels me to take the shot. I have just pressed the shutter release from six feet when a hand grabs my forearm. I turn around to encounter a woman's face outlined by a mourning veil.

"Do not photograph a blind person without asking," she says with conviction. "It brings bad luck—for both of you."

The woman is carrying a baby wrapped slingshot around her back. She cups her hand and raises it to my face. I wasn't expecting a beggar in this guise. I am unable to decipher whether her sorrowful expression is genuine or rehearsed. Finally I shake my head negatively, but she persists, chanting a painful litany as she follows. I cross the street rapidly and she stays on the other side, unwilling to risk her safety and the child's to the onrushing traffic.

I carry my cameras crisscrossed like bandoliers. The zoom lens attracts the most attention. Pedestrians step to one side, stop and stare at it with a mixture of curiosity and apprehension. At first this overreaction is puzzling, but as I walk further, I notice soldiers posted in front of banks, government buildings and at major intersections. They, too, seem wary of the 80-200; some shuffle their feet and stroke their weapons as I draw near. I conclude the barrel of the lens and the pistol-grip attachment must be as threatening to these people as the barrels of the soldiers' rifles, resembling a tear-gas launcher or something more deadly, a new weapon in the arsenal of repression perhaps. More than ever I am keenly aware of the many parallels between the acts of taking photos and shooting firearms. Both presume a sharp eye, in both a target is select-ed and its range found through a viewfinder; in both a spring mechanism is cocked and a trigger smoothly pressed, hopeful-ly before the victim has time to react.

The inherent fear of the population is revealed full force when I attempt to take the next exposure. A frail girl selling gum wants me to buy some. She is not at all shy, and even though she isn't the type of subject the agency ordered, she has an indigenous beauty I cannot disregard. I make a deal with her, agreeing to buy a pack if she lets me take her pic-ture. But as I am zooming in on her face, a black dress fills the viewfinder. A woman leads her away, keeping the girl protect-ed from the camera and gesturing angrily at me.

I reach the Plaza Mayor. It doesn't match very well the preconception I formed of it reading the description in the brochure. In my version there are many trees, flowers and bal-loon vendors around an ornate fountain. Instead there is a huge flag in the center that underscores the drab square's resemblance to a military parade ground, and the cathedral's lines are as harsh and fortress-like as those of the presidential palace on the opposite side. All around the arcade, political banners and giant blowups of the president stretch between columns. The soldiers guarding the square obviously belong to an elite unit. They goosestep in perfect phalangist formation and are outfitted in white helmets, gloves, and high boots. When they pass the presidential palace, they raise their arms in salute, though the balconies are empty.

I choose a table at an outdoor cafe and order a drink. As soon as the waiter leaves, two boys approach me with a boot-black box and offer their services. Reluctantly I show them that my shoes are made of a material that can't be polished. They appear deeply disappointed, so I toss them each a coin. The waiter thinks they are begging and chases them away from the premises.

I review my list of assignments. For the next three days I am expected to keep the whirlwind pace of a tourist, snapping shots of pyramids, temples, colonial churches and monasteries, museums and murals, never penetrating beyond the texture and pigmentation of the obvious. I consider the effect the images I sell will have on travelers, who might believe they're missing something really important if they fail to visit the sites pictured in the brochure. They will see what I suggest they see, and I in turn must see what the government pays me to see.

I decide to start my shooting assignment at the Zona Rosa. Though small in area, the district is prominently outlined in the map, its triangular shape tinted in bright pink. I read the paragraph devoted to it in the text:

> *La vie en rose*. There are no better words to describe the ambience of our ZONA ROSA. Romantic. Elegant. A secluded isle created for your pleasure. Shop for the latest fashions from Paris and Madrid. Browse through galleries where archeological treasures and avant-garde masterpieces are displayed side by side. Visit workshops where skilled silversmiths shape the precious metals of our fabled mines into custom jewelry. Later, dine in one of several establishments featuring continental cuisine at its most exquisite. Rekindle an old romance to the sensuous rhythms of a bolero at a rooftop nightclub. Be sure to include the Zona Rosa in your itinerary. And don't forget your camera. It's an experience you'll want to share with your friends back home.

I hail a taxi and ask to be driven there. We ride along a wide avenue reminiscent of European boulevards. Huge estates protected by wrought iron fences occupy entire blocks. Some are impeccably preserved pre-Independence mansions, others stunningly modern structures of steel and volcanic rock. In contrast to the parts of the city I've seen thus far, there are no street vendors or beggars here, though soldiers are equally omnipresent.

Just as the brochure promised, the sun is shining when we arrive at the Zona Rosa. Despite the diaphanous quality of the light, it will be difficult to prove on film the claims made in the brochure. But I earned the assignment precisely because I have a reputation for making the ordinary appealing, the plain attractive. For three hours I go about my business in a professional, uninspired manner, using a meter rather than intuition to judge the incidence of light, underexposing slightly to saturate bright colors, overexposing half a stop to bring out details of shaded façades or the dark complexion of storekeepers who pose stiffly as if sitting for a daguerreotype. Although I shoot over 50 frames, not once do I feel the thrill of capturing an elusive element of reality, withdrawing from it as soon as I press the shutter release.

I have a late lunch at one of the finer establishments of the Zona Rosa, compliments of the manager, who hopes I am partial to his restaurant in my selection of photographs. I let him know that it really isn't my decision, but he brings the best wine to my table all the same. I assure him I will present his business in the best light possible.

While I savor the superb mountain-grown coffee, I glance at the map once more and select some minor sites I can cover on my way back to the hotel. I trace out the coordinates and begin walking. The heavy meal and the altitude combine to make me somewhat dizzy, but I think I can cover the distance in less than an hour. It has gotten rather warm; many shops have closed down for the afternoon, and there's hardly any traffic.

Inadvertently I am drawn into streets that become narrower like funnels. In a matter of blocks I traverse several zones, leaving behind the Neoclassic, the Baroque, and the Romanesque eras, each in a more advanced state of decay than the preceding one. Gradually the structures deteriorate to amorphous masses of dark adobe that tilt at illogical angles. According to the map I should be nearing the Plaza Mayor, but somewhere I crossed the lines drawn by the government cartographers and entered a disturbing network of subhuman dwellings, a cubistic slum pieced together from a collective blueprint of need and despair. Around a ravine used as a landfill, a tent camp is thriving. The stench of a decomposing matter is overwhelming. Entire families and packs of dogs vie for anything edible in the piles of detritus. I am sickened by what I see, but more so by my complicity in the plot to paint a celestial vision of a city vastly more Hell than Heaven. For the first time in years, I allow my emotions to take over and I shoot desperately, painfully aware that no lens is sharp or wide enough, no film sensitive enough to record the depth of hopelessness I witness, ashamed to recognize that my mind has been a *camera obscura*, a latent image graveyard for pieces of reality void of human form or action, a lifeless extension of a viewfinder that relied on reflex to do it all. A mirror was raised, an x-volume of light rushed through the open diaphragm, a curtain closed, and the world remained at infinity. But now I am the focal point, I am the center of an image I can't escape. I can't awaken from this dream with coal-black militant eyes, with voices full of hatred screaming, "Yankee go home." If I could only explain, I want to run, but someone grabs me from behind, holds my arms back. The first blow

drives deep into my belly, pushing my intestines against the
pelvis with a heavy thud, the second one drops me to my
knees and now I am paralyzed, unable to beg for mercy, gasp-
ing for air as he rips the cameras off my shoulders and throws
them to the approving spectators. Thankful it's not my life
they want, I watch them smash the cameras against a wall,
shatter the lenses, pull the exposed film from the reel and set
it on fire. And when a boy steps forward to spit on my face, I
drift into darkness to a round of applause.

The Volunteer

...and I on this side, prisoner of another time...to not know who they were, that woman, that man, and that boy, to be only the lens of my camera, something fixed, rigid, incapable of intervention.

J. Cortázar, *Blow-up*

One year later the landscape retained its unnerving resemblance to a Rousseau in all its menacing primitiveness, and he felt as if a Heart of Darkness lay in ambush on both banks of the river. He was still a stranger, and it hadn't been difficult to imagine the unfinished road as an endless silent swell dragging the car, gathering sediment of human suffering each time a trail from the hinterland emptied into the mainstream, pushing its eternity of earth and blood relentlessly towards the sea. Once in a while the car would stop at a tributary of pain to take on another load of palpable misery. There was an infinite supply of that on the island, huge plantations that could be exploited for export if some enterprising missionary ever discovered the place. How deceitful to the air traveller who saw nothing but solid green rimmed in blue.

He had been the first passenger and had chosen to sit in the back and opposite the wheel to avoid the afternoon sun. But even though he was next to the window, not a breath of fresh air reached him. There were twelve passengers besides him now, including the two men riding in the open trunk with their squalid pig. It seemed as if the six passengers to his left were all crowding against his flesh to force him to feel their otherwise fragile presence. The air that entered the car circulated through their emaciated lungs and was left impoverished, contaminated with a fatalism that appeared inbred after so many generations of hopelessness.

The driver was no longer visible from his cramped position, but the volunteer could hear his reassuring, carefree whistling above the subdued talk of the peasants. This one was rather cheerful compared to the one he had met almost exactly one year before on the way from the capital to his assignment. Somewhere in his room he still kept a crumpled newspaper picture of Trujillo. It had been given to him by that first driver, a man who was convinced the Benefactor of the Fatherland was not dead but exiled and awaiting a popular uprising demanding his return to power. The image of the old dictator, the man had asserted, would serve as a safe-conduct in the inevitable turmoil and bloodshed. But this was a land doomed to no more revolutions. The Peace Corps and the Marines would see to that.

The volunteer struggled to unfold the map once again, arousing the curiosity of the peasant seated next to him. He showed the man the point where they should be. The distance to the coast from where he had started was roughly forty miles, yet they had just passed the town that marked the halfway point, and already they were well into the third hour of travel. He explained to the man that he was making a tour of the island. He traced out the routes carefully, reading the names of the towns out loud. The outside world was incomprehensible for these people, because ten square miles of rain forest was more than enough to crush them.

He planned to use his off-duty month traveling, to keep the monotony at a minimum. All the other volunteers in his group had decided to take their leave on the mainland. But he was afraid that if he left the country, he might never return. Looking back, he had accomplished nothing tangible in a year, unless one believed showing kids how to play basketball on a dirt court was an achievement of significance. He was supposed to be teaching teachers to teach better, although he himself had never taught before. But that's what the government had requested, and, first of all, volunteers were expected to be diplomatic. It would have made more sense to dig latrines for the entire town.

"I shit on the Lord," the driver cursed when the left rear tire began to wobble wildly. The two men in the trunk were almost thrown out, and the pig started to squeal pitifully as if sensing its impending sacrifice. Everyone was shaken out of a midafternoon stupor and leaned forward, tensely watching as the driver controlled the swerving and brought the overloaded car to a halt. A few hundred yards ahead there was a wooden bridge over a brook. Several huts had been erected around a clearing near the water. The driver told them to go wait in the shade, suggesting that perhaps they could buy something to eat from the families. The volunteer decided to stay and help change the flat. When the two men took the pig out of the trunk to let it roam, he realized there was no spare.

"Well, my friend, they say Americans are mechanical wizards. Here's your chance to show me it's true."

The driver was facing him, feet wide apart, grinning. He pushed back his incongruous sailor cap and crossed his arms, as if ready to witness a quick miracle. The volunteer appreciated his humor and smiled back.

"They call me Berto," the driver offered as he stepped forward and extended his arm. "You must think I'm crazy, not carrying a spare tire. Fact is, it got stolen last night. Damn kids get a lot of mileage out of an inner tube. They make rubbers out of them," he concluded, laughing joyously.

"Much pleasure," the volunteer answered, shaking his head in disbelief. "They call me Miguel here. By the way, you did a good job handling the blowout. We might all be in the ditch half-dead right now."

"It was easy," the driver said, shrugging off the compliment. "Happens all the time. Hey, you speak good Spanish. When the Marines came, they couldn't say anything except *hijo de puta* and *chinga tu madre*. This is a better idea to make friends for Yankee imperialism."

Both men laughed in complicity, establishing a tentative fraternal link.

The volunteer fetched two rocks to place under the front wheels while the driver proceeded to set up the jack. A few minutes later they had succeeded in loosening the rusted nuts, and the flaccid tire fell on the road, stirring a layer of dust.

"Now I'll have to wait for a ride back into town. After they patch it up, I might be able to get a ride back here. If we're lucky, we might get going in a couple of hours," the driver explained.

"Do you think the suitcase will be safe on the rack?"

"Oh hell, yes. These peasants don't have a use for one or for what's inside. I think you might as well go by the stream where it's cool and take a nap. I wouldn't eat or drink anything, though. You gringos got weak stomachs for all your toughness."

The volunteer started walking towards the bridge, leaving the driver who lay down under a small tree using the tire for a pillow. The silence made him feel lonely. Again the impression that the road was moving overcame him. It was like a strong current leading inexorably to a destiny he did not wish to reach. When he made it to the bridge, he held on to the decaying railing desperately, as if he were about to drown in a sea of stifling air. He concentrated on the swift stream below and regained his balance. He noticed a tree with wide, low protective foliage and decided to rest under it. As he was falling asleep, he absurdly remembered reading about the Admiral of the Ocean Sea, who thought he had landed in Japan because the aborigines called that region the Cibao, where gold and fabulous riches abounded.

⊙ʄʄ~

"Wake up, sir. Wake up."

A gentle hand timidly shook his shoulder. Visions of the Midwest scattered as he awoke; he couldn't perceive where he was or what language the child was speaking.

The boy persisted politely, afraid of a violent reaction. The volunteer squinted and the lush background inundated the last gray prairies of November that remained coherent.

A woman standing behind the kneeling boy was gesturing. He raised himself up on his elbows, his mind still heavy with confusion.

"You are from the North, aren't you?" the woman was asking.

He nodded meekly, intimidated by the tone of contained anger and desperation.

"Then you have to help me. The people there said you were in the Peace Corps. They say you must know some medicine."

The volunteer got to his feet. Everything had an unreal and alien quality to it. He was dizzy and had to lean on the tree to steady himself. He closed his eyes and breathed deeply.

"You must help me," the woman insisted. "Nobody around here knows what to do."

He opened his eyes and tried to understand what was happening. He glanced up the road where the car was and saw that the driver was gone. "You must come with me right now," the woman kept pleading. "My girl is very sick."

"You're mistaken. I don't know medicine. Besides, my car may leave any time now."

It was a very poor argument, but he was not able to reason well.

"Our house is not far. We can hear the motor when it starts," she countered.

The volunteer sensed he had fallen into an irreversible situation. The boy noticed his anxiety and hid his face in the mother's lap.

"You have to help. You are from the North. Her father was from the North, too."

It was hard to believe the woman, but that piece of information had tied him morally to the sick girl. He had no choice but to ask for more details, and that was tantamount to accepting the invitation.

"Did she have an accident?"

"No. It's something inside her. She doesn't sleep and she doesn't want to eat. Come and you will see. I want you to see her."

"All right. But you understand, I'm not trained in medicine. I'm afraid I won't be of much help."

The heat was blistering the road and his mind. Most of the passengers had formed a perfect semicircle around a tree and were worshipping it in their sleep. The pig had been tied to a stake in a muddy spot and was eating royal palm nuts as a last meal. Small patches of mandioc needed cultivation on both sides of the path, as did a stunted stand of maize. These transplanted sharecroppers from Andalusia had not thrived in the tropics. If they had any memory left, they probably would wish their ancestors had stayed in their whitewashed land, where the sharp contrasts made it easy to choose between life and death.

He had to stoop down to enter the thatched hut at the end of the footpath. It was quite dark inside, and from the packed dirt floor emanated a cool dampness that was surprising to the skin. He was amazingly conscious of his irises changing their aperture, searching for those rays that would illuminate his senses. He detected a glow in one corner of the room. The woman lit a candle and the glow became a shadow. All the humble objects in the one-room dwelling were enhanced to unbearable magnitudes by the dim light. The woman stood holding the wick, waiting for him to make a move. The volunteer approached the girl and stroked her hair. He was able to determine its color; it was blonde.

"Does it hurt somewhere?" was all he could ask. The tone of his voice resembled that of an old priest's in a confessional, a tired, impotent voice that forgave sins beforehand.

"*Puta*," she answered without looking up. She had said it slowly, with a controlled rage that didn't befit her age. The mother came forward and slapped her hard on the face.

"Don't you say that anymore. Don't you dare say that again," she screamed.

"*Puta. Puta. Puta.*"

Every time her mother slapped her, she repeated the word, distorting the pitch and stretching one of the vowels so that each utterance was completely different from the other. The volunteer divined she must have been raped. A rough chain of events unfolded intuitively, starting with an hysterical invasion to prevent a second Cuba from developing in the Caribbean, a Marine raping or seducing a woman during the

occupation, the cynical cropping up of recessive genes which
had been planted perhaps during another remote and now forgotten occupation or at some two-bit whorehouse near the
scum-filled port of Santo Domingo to form a being too tempting in this rotten paradise even at age nine or thereabouts.
Then he was struck by a crushing realization of futility. He
looked desperately for a redeeming experience in the past
year, but could only see himself sitting a few months before at
a whorehouse, drinking from a phallic one-foot tall bottle of El
Presidente beer while his *puta* played with his genitals.

He ran out. The mother and daughter were still hurting
each other rhythmically.

~⁂

"Don't worry about it, Miguel. There's nothing you or I or
anybody can do for that girl. You gringos, always trying to tell
the world what to do, one way or another," Berto said as he
lowered the car.

"But don't you see, I'm supposed to help people. That's
why I'm here. That's why we're all here."

The driver burst out in laughter.

"No, no, no. You can't change things. You're here for a
ride. Right now, you're going on a long ride with me, right?
Other volunteers go for longer rides, to Africa or Brazil, right?
That's why I think it should be called the Cuerpo de Paseo,
instead of the Cuerpo de Paz, don't you think?"

Berto laughed again. The volunteer didn't then, although
he understood the language very well.

Sea Grapes

It happened around the last days of summer vacation, after the national regatta that used to fill Varadero with all kinds of people from all over the country. In those days, regatta Sundays were like a carnival come to town; the buses and trucks would arrive before dawn overflowing with people, and as the sun rose the percussion of drum skins, maracas, and *claves* would wake us. I remember how much I liked to lie in bed as if hypnotized, mesmerized by the music that was pure rhythm, without melodies of any kind yet impregnated with the same primordial message as the downpours in the night. It's true that the Revolution has changed everything, and that there will never be regattas like the ones then, with the yachts that came from Havana, the old battleships that would steam offshore all day blowing their horns, and the huge feasts and drunken sprees that unfortunately always ended with someone drowning.

My folks had already bought me my new books and my uniform for parochial school: two white shirts and a pair of stiff khaki pants that had to last me the whole term. I had shot up quite a bit that summer, but my tie would have to do for another year. They also had to buy me new shoes; besides having grown, my feet had become flat from going barefoot so much. That was me. Marcelinito went to the public school and didn't need a uniform. But just the same he'd go to school all year wearing the same old pair of pants and the same cotton shirt. Chaquito didn't go to school. He'd go barefoot all year, even when the cold fronts came in from the North around Christmas, when the hotels were full of American tourists.

Chaquito's pants were always the same, rolled up to the knees so that the cuffs wouldn't get full of the sand and mud around Cayo Confite. His father was a cook in a hotel and spent all his money in Cárdenas, at the whorehouses.

I am writing this out of nostalgia, because Chaquito drowned and because Marcelinito and his family went away to the North, although that doesn't matter to me so much; because nothing's the same and at least by writing, something can be recaptured. I wish I could believe that by writing one could change the past as well as recover it. But the way I acted that day is irrevocable. I could make excuses, but that would be even more cowardly. At least it's somewhat quieting to know that what Chaquito and I did was the beginning of a liberation, the destruction of a monstrous myth that could have deformed my life forever. It's what I did afterwards that filled me with a shame that has lasted to this very day.

That afternoon, the three of us were running around without shirts, as usual. Marcelinito and I were almost black, as tan as our skin could get. But, still we were not dark enough to match Chaquito's. We had met by chance down at the pier on 54th Street, the one that was leveled years ago by a hurricane. Sometimes after a bad storm when the sands shift, you can still see two or three pilings, stuck there forever, jutting out from the bottom. It disturbs me to see that some dead tree trunks can outlast a person.

Marcelinito and I had just finished helping with the launching of the fishing boats that were leaving from 49th Street to fish for red snapper, taking advantage of the last quarter moon of the summer. We had gone down to the beach after the customary siesta to see if we could find some bottles to sell Luis, the Cantonese who owned the grocery. We didn't find any, so we had to be content with the *real*, the ten-cent piece Manengo gave us for helping them launch. Since we weren't strong enough to push like them, they put us in charge of the launching rod; when it came out by the stern we grabbed it and put it under the prow again and again until the boat rolled into the water.

After they put out to sea, we decided to walk up to 54th Street to see if by chance the tide had left a twenty-cent piece or *real* in the sand. As we approached 52nd Street, we recognized Chaquito at the end of the pier swirling his line and casting it into the surf, looking for blue runner. Marcelinito and I raced to the pier and I beat him easily. He was fat, the little bastard.

I asked Chaquito what he'd caught. He raised up a stringer to show us some runners glittering in the sun, still half-alive. His pants were all smeared with blood. One of the runners had swallowed the hook and Chaquito had used his bait knife to cut through the gills to get it out. He asked us what we were up to, and we said we were combing the beach for coins.

"I know where there's money," he said.

"Where?" we asked.

"I know where," was all he answered.

We sat there for a while arguing over what kind of bait was best to catch blue runner, whether it was a piece of lobster or a grouper fillet. Finally, we got tired of wrangling and Chaquito won; there was no one our age who could beat him in an argument. "So you're wasting your time combing the beach for money, are you?" He sat there thinking for a minute. "A couple of bucks wouldn't do me any harm, actually." He invited us to walk with him down the beach, and we accepted. He reeled the line onto the spool and put it in his pocket along with the makeshift bait knife that he had fashioned out of an old razor. He left the stringer in the water tied to a piling to keep the blue runners fresh.

"Hey, man, where are we going?" I asked him.

He said he didn't know, just to walk along the beach to see if we could find some money. "If you don't want to tag along, then hightail it home," he said.

It was still around four o'clock, and we wouldn't eat until six. That was at my house and at Marcelinito's. At Chaquito's they only had one meal at noon, and sometimes at night if his father brought something from the hotel. That's why he fished.

I recalled that Eulalia's son, Puya, had gotten a job at the Internacional, and it occurred to me to go see if he wouldn't let us sneak into the pool.

"O.K." Chaquito said, "that's where the money is anyway."

"Hey, what money?" Marcelinito asked him.

"None of your business, fatso. If you want, come on and you'll see."

I couldn't imagine what money he was talking about, and thought he was just bullshitting. We walked along with high hopes, Chaquito and I teasing the hell out of the fat bastard who was defenseless against the two of us.

"See my girlfriend here?" Chaquito would start off.

"How do I know she's your girlfriend, man?" I'd answer.

"Raise up her skirt and you'll see." Marcelinito almost cried with rage.

We went by Batista's house. You always went past his house with a little respect, with a little fear perhaps, like trying to hide a crime you never committed. Further on, all the houses belonged to the rich, with gardens that were watered year round and huge windows made of stained glass. The beach around there was completely deserted. Once in a while, we'd stumble across a paper cup or plate abandoned since the Sunday of the regatta. I was disheartened to think how there would be no more Sundays with hard sugar candy and *canip* vendors until June. Hopelessness was in the air, in the dry sand that the stiff breeze whipped up and plastered against your skin. Now I realize that it was hopelessness, but then I didn't know what that silence meant.

The fishing boats were way down the coastline, about as far as the old water tower, halfway between the Internacional and Dupont's mansion. Now they were no more than tiny dots disappearing behind the waves and bobbing up again like corks. It made your eyes dizzy just to look at them.

"The wind's really whistling this afternoon," Chaquito said, acting like somebody who knew a lot about fishing. "If the wind and the current don't square, they'll have to turn back."

I asked him how many times he'd gone fishing.

"Who me? Shit, hundreds of times. One time I went with Mongo la Jaba, once with Juruminga and..."

"Juruminga, the one who sucks his *pinga*," Marcelinito interrupted him. I'm sure the words must have slipped out, because he was chicken. But since Chaquito was like a godson to Juruminga, he didn't like it.

"Why don't you say it to his face like a man, you little homo."

I had to step in so that Chaquito wouldn't tear him apart.

"You heard what he said, Joseíto. Tomorrow I'll tell Juru when he comes back in."

"Don't tell him anything, man, he was just kiddin'," I said.

We were coming up to the hotel. The beach stretched out almost miraculously in front of the building to at least double its normal width. The sand was raked smooth and there was no trash. The sailboat was beached, the one Primo, the black man, used to rent for a buck an hour. In time, I made friends with him, and he took me out for rides when he had no business. I have no idea where he's gone now. The sailboat was destroyed by a norther years ago. There aren't any more tourists to rent sailboats to, anyway.

We went to the pool and whistled at Puya, who was trying to look real cool with his dark glasses, sunbathing like the Americans.

"What the hell are you kids doing here?" he asked us.

"Nothin'. Just walkin' along the beach. We came to see if you'd let us jump off the diving board."

Puya had it made at the hotel. He was Manengo's nephew, but he never did like to fish and was always looking for something else. Since he knew how to swim well, they had made him a lifeguard. After that, he always went around well-dressed and never lacked two or three pesos to go to the show and to the whorehouse in Cárdenas every week. He had promised to take me when I turned fourteen. "I'm going to teach you how to shoot it," he'd say to me.

Puya escaped with Manengo to Florida. You've got to have balls to risk crossing the channel in an eighteen-foot rowboat with a one-horse power motor. I heard he's somewhere around Chicago now, married to a rich old lady. He always did like the good life and money.

He told us he couldn't let us in. We tried to talk him into it, but he wouldn't even let us across the fence. Chaquito called him a piece of shit and started running. Marcelinito and I ran after him for fear that Puya would get mad. Chaquito kept yelling "piece of shit, piece of shit" as he ran, practically doubled over with laughter.

We passed by some gardens of tropical plants not native to Varadero. We went around the building, surveying it, and saw the tennis courts and the unbelievably green golf course.

"That's a game for sissies," Chaquito said after observing two old men who were playing. "You'd have to be a real prick to stand there with a stick and hit a little ball around all day long."

We soon got bored watching the old men and went back toward the side of the beach. There we found Graciel with his box of shells. His father no longer fished because of some illness or other. So, to earn a little something he made necklaces and little dolls from shells which Graciel sold to the tourists. Back then, he was a quiet kid, behaving as if he were embarrassed to be alive. He always went around with his navel exposed to the wind as if it were demanding some of the nourishment his mother had not been able to properly provide for him. I say this because before the Revolution there was plenty of hunger in Varadero. Fortunately, in my house we always had a plate of rice and beans, but I know of many who had to get by with bread and brown sugar when the weather was bad or the fish weren't biting.

I asked him what he had sold.

"Nothin'. Seventy-five cents' worth."

"With that you won't even eat scraps tonight," Marcelinito told him. I don't know why he said that. It was a pretty shitty thing to say. But it seemed to me that he said it viciously.

"What the fuck is it to you, you fat piece of shit?" All at once Chaquito had leaped in front of Marcelinito, ready to strike. "Just because his old man owns a shitty little store, he thinks he's better than everyone else. You little bastard, I'm going to bash your face in."

Marcelinito got scared. "I was just kiddin'," he said.

I had to step in again; I didn't want to see any blood. "Next time I'll let him smash your face in, so you better watch out," I said. I should have let Chaquito kill him right there.

Chaquito cooled off, and we went up to the lobby windows. We could see our reflection in the Plexiglas, as if we ourselves were on the inside of the lavish parlor. It was full of ornaments and things we couldn't name; things whose function we couldn't even imagine. I know now that material things are nothing more than another illusion, but then the magnificence of manufactured objects from the North somehow made me feel that we were inferior to the Americans. We moved away from the windows, dazed.

"Primo says that a room here costs twenty bucks a night," Graciel informed us.

"Fuck. My old man don't make that in a week," Chaquito replied. Then he added, "All Cayo Confite would fit in here," and he began to shout at the building something he himself had made up: "I'm from Cayo Confite, the barrio of the bed pans, the isle of turds." We just about died from laughter, but in view of what happened later, it's easy to understand that beneath that laughter there was a strange pride in his world of poverty. More than anything, what he was shouting was a threat to the imposing Internacional and what it represented.

We were thirsty, so Graciel took us to a tap hidden behind some oleander bushes. We let the warm water that was coiled in the hose run out and drank our fill of fresh water. We rolled in the grass to rest a while, and Chaquito said he felt like masturbating. "Jesus, you are filthy," Marcelinito told him. He didn't pay any attention.

He crawled over and hid between the wall and the bushes. We waited for him. A few minutes later, he came out buttoning up his pants. "I came right away," he said. I had already forgotten about the money business and was getting hungry.

We decided to go back, but Graciel wanted to stay and see if he couldn't sell anything else when the guests came out for a swim at sunset. We went down toward the water's edge to where the sand was firmer. "Looks like it's gonna be a good fishing night; the wind has died down a little," Chaquito said. "And the skies are clear," he added. The sun was already over El Pan de Matanzas; the beach stretched out to the west like an infinite humid tongue.

This was very same beach that I'm standing on now. But today the colors aren't as crisp as they were then. I myself don't seem to be as alive. Or maybe it is just that reality has been fading away. Still, I have yet to speak about the break-in. The sun will set over El Pan within one half-hour, just like that evening, and if I leave for Havana tonight I may never finish telling this story.

I remember that we picked on Marcelinito again and that we pelted him with wet sand balls until we made him cry; that we jumped in the water to rinse off and pee. Without realizing it, we had gone beyond the beach houses of Jabón Candado, and a block further on there was a house that belonged to an American who only used it during the winter. The rest of the year it was locked up, indifferent to time and weather.

"I feel like stealing some grapes," Chaquito said. I knew immediately that he was referring to the American's caletta tree. It was known to produce the sweetest grapes in Varadero, another of those ironies that became evident as I began to acquire a political conscience. We jumped over the wall with no problem except for Marcelinito, who was afraid of the gardener and didn't dare. We should have let him go home.

"What fucking gardener are you talking about, Marcelinito? You think someone's gonna be watering the grass at this hour, you piece of shit." Marcelinito was silenced.

The caletta tree was loaded. It was the season for sea grapes and *hicacos*. We made cones from caletta leaves and filled them with the ripe grapes. Then we sat down to enjoy them and shoot the bull.

"Here's where the money is," Chaquito said at last.

I had it figured out, but it didn't occur to me at that instant that I had.

"Joseíto, do you dare?" the challenge came wrapped in the question.

Once I had carried off a diving mask someone had left on the beach, but that was nothing compared to what Chaquito wanted to do. I felt fear; it was one of those few sensations that one never forgets, that you can almost exactly recreate by thinking back on the experience. But in spite of the fear, I understood I was going to be Chaquito's accomplice; it was a fate I couldn't escape.

"I won't even ask you because I know you'll chicken out," he told Marcelinito.

"You stay here outside and whistle in case anyone comes." He ordered me to bring him a coconut. When I gave it to him, he said, "I'm going to get enough out of here to buy some clothes and go to the whorehouse."

He broke a window with the coconut, and the shattered glass fell inside. He went in first, and then helped me get through; I still don't see how we didn't cut our feet. I noticed that next to the dry taste of fear another sensation like pleasure was coming to life, something similar to what you feel when you risk your life driving at high speeds.

The house was dark. I didn't want to turn on the lights for fear that someone might notice, but Chaquito switched them on. We remained motionless for a while, observing furniture that we had only seen in the movies. What caught my attention most at first was a wall filled with books; I had never imagined that there could be so many books together. Chaquito sat down on the sofa and began to bounce up and down while I leafed through some magazines in English that had many color pictures. He managed to open up a piece of furniture that turned out to be a record player. We messed around with it until we got it to work and put on the first record from the pile.

"Hey, what kind of garbage is that, man? Joseíto, don't you know how to speak English? I do, listen: *Americano, cano, cano, you gotti moni, foki foki.*" He said that dancing to the beat of the record. He kept on saying foki foki and began to explore the house.

"Joseíto, come here and look at the john." I remember that the bathroom was all done in blue tile and that it was bigger than the living room in my house.

"How the fuck do you take a shit here, man? This is too much." He turned on the faucets in the shower and let the water run. "Let's see if this damn place floods."

In the medicine cabinet, we found an electric razor and grabbed it. We were going to need something to put the things in, so we went into a bedroom and pulled a pillow case off a pillow. Little by little, my fear subsided. By now I didn't even think about someone finding us. I grabbed the bedspread and threw it on the floor, obeying I don't know what impulse. Chaquito threw himself on the bed and said, "This is good; you could fuck on this all night long." There was an alarm clock on the night table and I put it in the pillow case.

"Say, where does that door go to?" he asked.

"That's a closet," I answered. I'd seen one in my aunt's apartment in Havana.

"A what?" he asked again.

"It's a little room to keep clothes in," I explained.

He opened the door, and we found ourselves in pitch-black darkness. We waited till our eyes got used to the dark so we could find the light switch. There were a few clothes, a yellow sportscoat, some shirts, and a pair of shoes. "This is for my old man," he said, and put two or three shirts in the pillow case.

We left the bedroom, and in the hallway, Chaquito picked up a big vase and smashed it on the floor. "I did that because it made my balls feel good," he said. He did it because he didn't understand the reason for those objects unknown in Cayo Confite.

Hatred was overflowing from his eyes; his actions were originating from something other than the need to steal. In the kitchen, after choosing a few pieces of silverware for his mother, he shattered many glasses and plates. I was contaminated by his fury and helped him with the destruction. Without really knowing it, we were ridding ourselves of the humiliation suffered at the hands of material objects. We moved to the living room; there we broke lamps, tipped over the bookcase, threw records against the wall. We turned over furniture and tore down the venetian blinds. Finally, we got over our rage, and fear began to creep in. We left like a bolt of lightning.

The sun had already set behind El Pan. We didn't find Marcelinito anywhere. We figured he'd gone home in a panic. We walked quickly along the darkened beach, silently, until we got to the pier, where we stopped to pick up the stringer of blue runner. "What do you want," he asked me, "the alarm clock or the electric razor?" I answered I wanted nothing, that I didn't need anything. Fear had taken hold of me and I wanted to free myself from the whole affair. "O.K., that's up to you. A lot of good they'll do me; we don't even have electricity in my house." I suggested he could sell them. "I'll see what I can do," he said.

I waited as he went to fetch the stringer. Then we split up. "I'm going to go through the empty lots on 46th Street," he said. That was the last thing I heard him say. There were no street lamps on those blocks and he could get to Cayo Confite without anyone spotting the bundle. I saw him for the last time that night fading into the darkness, the stringer dancing at the side of his body like a bricklayer's plumb, the pillow case rolled up under his arm.

I found myself totally alone, feeling cold. I had to make up a tale before returning home. That was the first night I was going to be late for supper and, somehow, I had a feeling that things would change from then on.

That night I told at least two lies. One to my folks; the other to Sergeant Alzugaray. Marcelinito had really chickened out when he heard us breaking things, and spilled the beans to his parents that we were stealing. Maybe he did it to get even, because we had worked him over so much that day.

I told the police that I had only eaten some sea grapes, and that they could search me if they wanted. And since I was the son of more or less decent parents, they didn't do anything to me, although I'm sure that neither the police nor my folks believed me. They sent Chaquito to the reformatory in Matanzas for six months. He escaped and then got sentenced for a year. When he came back, we kept being friends, but he had become embittered. He could no longer be the same. Neither could I, because I had learned the power of a lie. In time, I decided to fight for a more just society, although between Chaquito and me, he was the real revolutionary, nonconforming until the end. The sea swallowed him when he tried to make his way to Florida in a stolen boat.

I am sitting here on this desolate beach trying to guess the exact moment when Chaquito drowned as he tried to jump across the sea. And, I imagine myself in Florida where my parents and so many of the others who left have made their home. I sit on the same sand that was here when the North was a crushing myth that made my eyes follow the trajectory of the planes flying to Miami. The sand is the same, but how things have changed. Perhaps some day all or most of them will return, like caguama turtles, in search of the shells they left buried here.

Rambles

The thin, forlorn-faced man pulled a chair out from under a rusty Cinzano table; wiped the pigeon droppings with a page torn off a yellow stenopad; arranged his bony butt on the wooden seat; invoked the muses that inspired Picasso, Miró, and Dalí; uncapped his lucky green ballpoint; and began to scribble:

The Ramblas are distinctively divided into four commercial segments. The first one, sloping seaward from the great Plaza, is devoted to the cultural enhancement of a deprived populace, as attested by the numerous book-and-newspaper stands that jam the two blocks. There's a proliferation of erotic literature, a veritable boom of Koka Shastras and pseudo-medical sex manuals, which prove to the sophisticated, beyond-the-Pyrenees visitors that after decades of planned domestic tranquility and economic growth, people in Spain need to be taught how to do it again.

The next section is the much-photographed, much-water-colored, much-pastelled section of birds and flowers, so why write about it.

Then come the café tables with the colorful canvas parasols and the dignified waiters who artfully soak perspiration off their necks with a simile of a smile.

Finally, at the end of the promenade and nearest the port, you find the Rambla de las Putas, where painted women answer "two, three, four thousand pesetas" when someone asks them their names, and who for roughly the equivalent price of an illustrated Koka Shastra, will perform any act pornographically described therein.

He put the pen down, satisfied with the tentative physical setting of his story. It was a start. A character has to have a medium in which to ambulate, just as a person must have circumstantial evidence of his existence. For the mind can't cope with pure abstractions; it needs concrete points of reference to construct a sturdy maze. He determined, then, that the center of the character's world would be in the third segment of the Ramblas at that particular table where he sat comfortably under the shade of whatever trees line the Ramblas.

He knew that a character has to act to create the illusion of life, so he had him order garlic mushrooms and a demi of a fine indigenous wine to stimulate his sensual perceptions and reactions.

A character also needs a chronology just as a real person does, since neither can escape the limitations of time and space. So to set the record straight, he wrote that he had arrived by train the day before after a long journey across many real or imagined borders, checked in at a hotel a block off the Ramblas, slept fifteen hours, shit-shaved-and-showered, went to a bank to make change, bought a pad at a bookstand, and set about the task of drawing his coordinates.

He was making progress until he arrived at the point where another character would be useful because it is cumbersome to bring out the thoughts when you are dealing with one single person. You need a looking glass to reflect upon, at least one, otherwise the story becomes an incomprehensible interior monologue with no credible witness to transcribe it, or a mere meaningless report of gestures. Then he decided to wait until a suitable woman sat down at a nearby table. And this didn't take long since it was the peak of tourist season.

They played the eye game till they both were sure the other was playing the game. Then he invited himself over, but she pretended she wasn't playing the game.

He knew this was part of the game, so he sat down and she was pleased he understood the rules so well.

"Name's Julius," he said.

"Mine Göni," she countered.

Literary characters have no sex, but readers are gullible and will believe one is male if it's called Julius and one female if it calls itself Göni, though both of them were lying, as he well knew, because he was Julius and his name was not a lie.

"I'm not married," he offered.

"Me neither," she countered. "Free as a cuckoo bird."

"You mean you're an adulteress?"

"Yes. I like to nest in other birds' nests."

This was hardly a model of verisimilitude, but all dialogues are so contrived. In fact, the more realistic they sound, the less credible they are. That was an axiom he'd discovered years back studying a foreign language via the audio-lingual method.

"In that case, I'm married," he admitted.

"So much the better."

Now here is a case of two characters of unknown nationality in a story set in Catalonia speaking English, yet no one objects to the artifice, mainly because the readers are likely to be English speakers and take it for granted that theirs is the dominant language.

"Are you really not married?" he asked in a tone of believing disbelief.

"I have a daughter."

"I see. Where is she?"

"I left her with some shepherd friends the other side of the Pyrenees."

"Of course."

"And you? Have you any?"

"Two, that I know of."

"Ha, ha, ha."

"I don't fool around."

"So I see."

Julius wrote down the preceding dialogue not so much to preserve its integrity as to needle her curiosity.

"What are you doing?"

"Do you care?"

"Depends."

"Do you know the difference between a film and a video?"

"Hmmm."

"I'm trying to develop a new writing technique."

"I knew it! You're a writer!"

"If you want to believe it."

"I've always wanted to meet one. Is it true that your penises are as tricky as your pens?"

"That's a good one. I'm impressed. Let's just say that both my pens are well sharp-ended."

"O là là."

"Coitus, orga sum."

"Ho, ho, ho."

This nonsense went on for an undetermined length of time, but to summarize that first, gratuitous tête-à-tête, Julius and Göni came to like each other rather well, as was to be expected since it was necessary for the further development of the narrative. They agreed to rendezvous at nine that evening for the customary apéritif in preparation for the ensuing répast et soirée and whatever else might develop.

Three hours later, Julius woke up feeling much refreshed. This national pastime of the siesta was very useful, instead of one draggy day you could have two. Darkness had set in, and he fumbled in it till he found the switch to the anemic lamp. When he was able to see, he discovered a pad next to the pillow.

There was something scribbled on it about him having a date with this woman at nine. It was already eight, so if he wanted to be presentable and on time, he must hurry.

He dressed nervously. It had been a while since he'd felt such excitement. Imagine impersonating a personage named Julius. He could do whatever he pleased without feeling remorse. He was not responsible for his actions. The author was. Anything goes, anything. Oh freedom! Freedom to forni-cate, fellatio and fantasize, unrestrained, unbridled, un-planned. "Free!" he shouted at the perplexed clerk as he passed by the desk. "*Libre*," he whispered to the sleepy door-man. "Fuck you," he informed to a bunch of *guardias*. "I love you," he said to an Andalusian gay with dreamy eyes. "I am that I am," he said to himself as he sat down at the Cinzano table and then ordered artichokes and beer.

He wrote:

My name is Julius, but that doesn't mean I am Julius.

I am that I am, no more and no less.

I have no a priori knowledge of myself and no destiny, only a reality scratched on a pad.

I drink beer, I eat artichokes, I see lights, and I hear a strange language about me.

I like French flicks because the heroes and heroines are always trying to *recommencer*.

As if one could really begin anew, the fools.

But it is fun to try.

It is fun to pretend being the creature and the creator.

The director and the actor with no script to follow.

The Father and the Son enraptured with their Likeness and no Holy Spirit to disturb their symmetry with Immacu-late Conceptions.

To be smoke without a cigar.

An ejaculation without a penis.

An orgasm without an ejaculation.

"In summary, what you want is an effect without a cause," interjected the lady leaning over his shoulder.

"Merde."

"What's wrong?"

"Here's a case of the unavoidable intentional fallacy."

"I don't understand what you mean."

"I mean that I meant to mean that Julius wanted to espouse a cause without effects, but somehow it got all twisted around and it took female intuition to show what I really meant."

"Let's go eat."

"Can't. Can't leave the paradox unresolved."

"We can think of something as we go along. I can help."

"But who are you, anyway?"

"Don't you remember? I'm Göni."

"No, but Julius was supposed to meet you at nine."

"Then you must be Julius, because it is nine."

"Good, good."

Julius clapped and the waiter who waited on them in the afternoon came out, but Julius didn't recognize him because he had exchanged his white uniform for a black one and his black wig for a white one.

After leaving a significant pourboire, Julius led his date into a side street. It was thrilling plunging with a stranger into a strange dateless world. Famished dogs dug in the detritus thrown out the balconies. At day's end land-sick sailors stopped at corners, unable to get their bearings from celestial navigation. Suspect men slid out of doorways to offer contraband, jewelry, and dope. An occasional bordello displayed archaic douches and other exotic paraphernalia in its show window.

"Tell me you are afraid," Julius begged his companion.

"I'm afraid."

"Let me hold your hand."

How many years had it been since he'd held the hand of a woman other than his wife's. It was like reliving adolescence, but this time it was real, not one of those imaginative nightmares in which the woman with whom he was having an affair turned out to be his wife or his mother-in-law.

"Göni, Göni."

"Yes?"

"I'm in love with your name. It's so sensuous!"

"You think so?"

"Absolutely. All fricative sounds are aphrodisiacal."

The harbor must have been so very close. Foghorns howled like lost animals calling their mates. The dense salt air crystallized in their throats, giving their voices a raspy quality and their bodies a thirst for things unknown. A café opened its swinging doors, and they accepted the invitation. It was noisy, it was dirty, but it was well-lighted and full of life. Clam shells and other discarded crustacean vestments crunched in the sawdust under their feet. The stench of decaying seafood frying in olive oil was overwhelming. A flamenco guitarist rolled *soleares* in a corner, and they sat near him so Julius could translate the enigmatic amorous laments improvised by sephardic Jews and gypsies centuries before.

"What would Ernest order in a situation like this?" Julius wondered.

"How about octopus or squid?"

"Yes, yes! They go so far back in evolution that our appetite for them shows our deep-rooted aversion to civilization. A splendid choice. Write that down."

At this point Göni protested because she didn't want to be relegated to the role of stenographer, so Julius agreed to let her claim co-authorship. After all, without her the story would have ended on page four, and he would have been nothing more than a truncated figment of the imagination.

The octopus was terribly rubbery, but the Valdepeñas was earthy and cheap. They ingested five, possibly six, carafes while Julius attempted to decipher the *saetas* and *soleares* that spoke of good love, bad love, adulterous love, suicidal love, but always of passionate love.

After a couple of undiluted hours of wine and flamenco, their swollen spirits were soaring with desire. The plan was working. He could feel her flesh blossoming like lotus flowers. The time was ripe so he placed a large bank note inside the guitar case in appreciation of the genuine artistry to which they had been subjected. True flamenco cannot be reproduced in the studio. One must have the tragic atmosphere of a proletarian *cafetín,* as Ernest so well understood.

The waiter brought the check scribbled on a piece of brown paper or rough toilet tissue. It's a perfect night for love, he winked knowingly. Seafood is rich in certain juices that promote virility. Have fun, my friend, I truly envy you.

On the way out, Göni pushed the swinging doors a bit too hard, and they smashed Julius on the forehead, opening a naughty gash over his right eyebrow which spilled blood on his shirt before his femme tenderly stopped the flow with a mini tampon.

An impartial observer would describe their gait as comical, for they were quite tipsy and feeling each other shamelessly. They could not wait much longer. Their hotels were too far and the streets too narrow for a taxi to conveniently appear. So they stopped in front of the first *pensión* they stumbled upon.

Now anyone who has been to old Barcelona knows that in order to gain entrance into a dwelling after sleepy-time, one has to stand at the door and clap vigorously. Soon an old man,

called a *sereno,* comes dragging his crippled legs and a chain
full of medieval keys. Said man, for a few pesetas, will open
the gates to Hell if necessary. It is a quaint way of employing
Civil War veterans and gored bullfighters.

The old hag who was in charge came out of her den stink-
ing of garlic and onions. She demanded proof of matrimony. It
was the only proper thing to do in a Catholic nation. God
might be hiding under the bed and not approve of such a carnal union. But Julius calmed her conscience by claiming they
were brother and sister touring, and by paying double of what
the bed and bidet were legally worth.

They stumbled up the four flights, giggling all the while.
They were sinners and they knew it, defying God Himself who
was hiding under the mattress with the bedbugs. Yoohoo,
Lord, we know You're in there even though You're invisible
like a Nineteenth Century narrator. That's all right. Voyeurs
don't bother us. You have to get Your kicks, too. We understand. We'll even leave the lights on so You can see better,
You Primordial Peeping Tom.

"Show me your pudenda," Julius begged as soon as he
found the light switch.

"You show me yours first," Göni riposted.

"I'm embarrassed."

"Now now. Why should you be?"

"I have varicocele."

"What's that? A venereal disease?"

"No, no. Medically speaking it is simply a varicose condition of the veins in the spermatic cord."

"Let me see, let me see!"

Julius pulled down his pants as self-consciously as the
time at the induction center during the war. It had been so
humiliating to bare his anomaly in front of so many fellows,

but he had the last laugh because the physician mistook it for a disqualifying hernia and kept him from being drafted.

"Oh, my God!" Göni gasped.

"I warned you."

"Let me feel it, let me feel it."

"Okay, but do it carefully."

Julius turned his head and coughed while Göni squeezed the inflamed scrotum.

"It feels like a bag of worms," she remarked happily. "In all my years of adulterous practice, I have never seen anything quite like it."

"I have a theory," Julius ventured timidly.

"About your balls?"

"Yes. I think the extra veins engorge the corpus with so much blood that it allows for a harder, longer erection."

"Prove it with deeds, mon amour, deeds, not words."

A detailed description of a sexual encounter would only result in the censorship of the story, so we'll fast forward a few hours to find Julius waking up for the third time in less than twenty-four, except that now he wasn't alone. What a wonderful feeling of fulfillment! After so many years of matrimonial celibacy, his wife would forgive him, wouldn't she? He was only human, and all men have to prove their prowess at least once during their mid-career crises. This rationalization appeased his conscience.

He indulged in the pleasant recreation of the events leading to the climax. They had played the mystical game Love is God and He is everywhere, behind the ears between the toes under the armpits, in the vagina. Of course, just the thought of it tickled his libido, and he reached for Göni, caressed her lithe body under the linen expecting it to respond like a modern dancer's. But she was in deep sleep, so he slipped his hand under the sheet and felt a pillow! He was caressing a pillow!

Where did she go? Julius jumped out of bed and flipped on the light, but found nobody, no trace of her clothes on the chair, nothing. She had left while he slept. But, why Göni? Why? He dressed himself, trembling like a child. Not again, God! He examined the bed for any unusual excretions that might provide a clue. It couldn't have been another one of his patented dry, wet dreams that he began experiencing after the vasectomy, could it?

He cried, "Göni, Göni. Where are you? Come back. I need you. Without you I don't exist."

Looking under the sheet once more, he found the yellow pad. It was true, not a dream. It was all written down—the rendezvous at nine, the plunging into the gothic world of old Barcelona, the flamenco, the *sereno*, the *pensión*, the last words. Deeds not words, words, words…

His world had crumbled, and he had come to the old one seeking reassurance in its repeatedly rebuilt permanence. And in the orderly gardens, he knew the irrigated Costa del Sol would be regenerating all along. And in the security afforded by a servile society spoonfed by the arranged incestuous marriage of Church and State; and in the predictable behavior of its subjects, mesmerized by the benign Mediterranean summer; and in the countless coves where fishermen, drowned in sunlight, mended centuries-old nets whose original twine had been entirely replaced by nylon, though it was nonetheless the same deadly mesh strengthened by a modern fabric; his body too mended itself continuously, but if it grew old instead, it would crumble in much less that one half century and could not be handed down like a fisherman's legacy. And although he was now here in the Ramblas buffeted by the saltpetered breeze, his mind was still crumbling, and he felt like the Cervantes character who thought he was made of glass and would shatter at the slightest collision. And after a fifth glass of wine, he cried, "Oh, reason, oh, reason why has thou forsaken me! I am that I am no more!" He took his shirt off, and before he could undo his pants, an agent of the state appeared out of the blue Mediterranean sky, grabbed him by the arms, and stripped him of his expired passport.

Steppes

To be or not to be a soldier, that was a question. To become a green marine or to escape in a yellow submarine. To drop acid with Tim or to drop the bomb on Ho Chi Minh. To burn your draft card in the park or to burn Viet Cong with napalm. To search and destroy gooks in rice paddies or to research books in libraries. But to question or not to question: That was, is, and forever shall be the question.

It was the best of times, it was the worst of times. Yesterday life wasn't such an easy game to play, but oh how I long for yesterday. Oh where, where have all the flower children gone, long time ago. Where, oh why, have you gone, Abbie Hoffman, yesterday. It all went so suddenly, a state of mind jolted and gone away.

Forgive me, but I cannot help the way I am, the way I look at things through a glass darkly no matter how bright the sun; nothing escapes the enzymes of my acid tongue, the corrosive juices of my gut reactions. The main reason my wife left me was my gloom-and-doom attitude, as she put it; the way I criticized everything from the President's foreign policy to her penchant for ruining hose on a daily basis. In another age, in another society, I may have served a purpose. But no one wants to be awakened from their upscale dreams to be warned of the possible derailment of their smooth-running bourgeois express.

⊙ﬀﬀ~

Among all the distinguished and tenured minds of a prestigious university, the one that influenced mine most belonged
to an obscure custodian from the Russian steppes. His name
was not Vladimir, but in order to protect the privacy of his
widow and for a more expedient, literary reason I shall refer
to him as Vladimir.

We exchanged our first words one fall evening in the
fourth floor men's room of _____ Hall, the Humanities building of a major midwestern university where I was a graduate
student in Comparative Literature and he, a night janitor. At
first I resisted his overtures to conversation. I had a fellowship to do research, and his visits to the small office I shared
with two ever-absent, ever-stoned fellows detracted from my
duties. But after a few of his narratives I looked forward to
the time he'd finish his chores on the fourth floor and join me
for coffee. The stories he told from the Old World cut through
the language barrier like an archetypal double edge. In those
days his mind was still sharp, though quickly deteriorating
from a nightly pint of vodka chased by however much Thun-
derbird it took to anesthetize it. An unpolished Nabokov, he
was able to mock in broken English the inconsistencies of his
adopted fatherland with crude but pulverizing observations.
To those who may not follow the Nabokov analogy, may I suggest stripping *Lolita* of sex in your next reading. You might
discover that instead of a tempting tale of tardy tenderness, as
one no doubt older reviewer with fantasies of his own inter-
prets the work, it is one of the most acid reactions to the
American Way ever expressed in writing.

To repeat myself, I was a doctoral candidate in Comparative Literature. My dissertation, left unfinished like so many
projects from the sixties, dealt with a Cuban movement of
absurdist fiction that preceded the post-Castro social realism.
It was the artistic freedom unleashed by the revolution that

made this movement possible, and though this had nothing to do with literary research, I was very much interested in the subject and wanted to understand why within two years the revolution was denying the freedom to write "defeatist and reactionary" literature. Vladimir provided me with an insight. Revolutions, to paraphrase him, do not exist beyond the spontaneous struggle that overthrows the established order, and the new intelligentsia takes itself too seriously to allow the possibility that life may be meaningless. Vladimir should know. He had survived several upheavals, including *the* Revolution.

At the time I was waging my own struggle for having requested a third student deferral. There was absolutely no way I could rationalize my worth to society as an apprentice literary critic any longer. I despised most of my professors and had come to agree with Governor Wallace that the majority of academes use briefcases to brown bag their peanut butter sandwiches. I had sunk to such a low level of self-esteem that I defaced my Master of Arts diploma by inserting an apostrophe between the letters of the preposition and then connecting the f to the Arts with a hyphen.

Yet I was reluctant to give up the academic life. I sensed that those of us fortunate to be on campus during the late sixties were in the midst of a Golden Age that would not be replicated in our lifetime. It was romantic to be alive; it was a period of great expectations and experimentation, hardly any of the latter empirical. Lyndon Johnson had decreed the American Pie to be of Texas proportions, and enough of his Great Society bribe eluded the bureaucracy to end up in unlikely hands. Our campus was, consequently, full of extraordinary characters whose least interest lay in scholarly pursuit. One could walk into a beer joint any evening and find someone plotting the Great American novel or ways to dismantle the very structure that made his idleness possible. *Ubi sunt*, I'd like to know, the Marxist radicals and the black militants, the jazz musicians who jammed at the Gaslight every Wednesday night, the promising poets who won the English Department contests. Oh where, where have all the flower children gone, long time passing. When nostalgia drives me to a college campus on a rainy fall afternoon and I confirm that America's obsession with plasticity, so poignantly symbolized by the neon sign in *Lolita*, is now manifested by the love of video games, I am painfully reminded of one of Vladimir's last lucid statements: "A movement fermented by the boredom of excess materialism instead of hunger—he said with characteristic pessimism—will not be a revolution but simply a revolt."

There were other reasons why I hadn't severed my ties to academia. The university was a refuge from a society unwilling to fully admit a refugee who showed too much otherness. I carried a card that certified me as an alien, by definition "one excluded from some group, an outsider." The adjective connotation given by the same dictionary, "repugnant," succinctly expresses how one is perceived by the general public. Forced into solitude at an age when most of my peers engaged in mutual masturbation, I discovered literature.

The proud recipient of a fellowship, I entered graduate school armed with a fervent belief in the power of the word to reveal deeper realities, be these personal or universal, and to transform mankind for the better. Since I believed that literature was valid only as an activity that shed light on the human condition, I found myself rebelling from the very first lecture against the trend to dehumanize it, to make of it no more than a linguistic exercise with no meaning beyond the text. I was disturbed to the point of incoherence whenever one of those shallow critics minimized the importance of the author, asserting that the artist was a tool that served the grand scheme of language instead of the opposite. They were like the Cuban officials who demanded that writers serve the scheme of their "revolution." They were jealous of the creator, so they systematically researched and destroyed.

The friendship between Vladimir and me deepened into affection as Indian summer decayed into fall. My peers didn't understand the relationship, for on the surface we didn't have much in common. He was a good thirty-five years older than I, we were from opposite ends of the world, he liked to drink and I preferred to smoke dope. But the fact we were immigrants superseded all other considerations. We discovered in each other a deep-rooted fear of not belonging and a profound longing for our homelands, which with all their imperfections we remembered as Paradise.

Wanting to know more about the Russian character, I had checked out a collection of stories by Chekhov. One story in particular caught my attention. Appropriately titled "In Exile," it juxtaposed the characters of an old man who had given up all hope in life and a young man who desperately clung to ideals no matter how hopeless they appeared. I was somewhat troubled by the parallels I saw between the fictional construct and our situation. Like the young Tartar, I still nurtured hopes of returning home someday, but Vladimir, like the old man condemned to row the barge eternally across the river, had lost hope of ever setting foot on the motherland again, a realization that filled his pale blue eyes with a glaze of sorrow. And like the old man in the story, the palliative for his infinite sadness was alcohol.

I didn't suspect how strong his dependence was until Vladimir invited me to dinner for the first time in October. Anticipating a tasty meal, something I didn't enjoy often as a bachelor, I treated myself to a reefer as I traversed the autumn-emblazoned campus. My appetite rose to a crispiness

that matched the late afternoon's air, and I stopped to buy a
bottle of Ruffino Chianti at a liquor store located just outside
university proper. I was feeling pretty good when Vladimir
answered the doorbell, but he was in higher spirits. He greet-
ed me effusively and introduced me to his wife Elga as if I
were a beloved nephew back from a long journey. We sat down
to a neatly prepared table covered with a variety of dark
breads, cheeses, crisp vegetables, and herring. In no time
Vladimir and I polished off a fifth of Smirnoff. I watered mine
down, but he drank it straight in small, frequent sips. At six
o'clock he turned on the TV to the Lawrence Welk show. He
asked Elga to dance and I watched them waltz elegantly
around the small living room, lost in their memories. The
polka number brought them back to reality and they grabbed
me by the arms. We stomped to Myron's accordion noisily,
arms locked in a circle.

The physical activity aroused our appetite. Elga joined us
in drinking the Chianti with the main dish, a hearty, well-
stocked stew. This was followed by cake and Turkish-style coffee; the resulting high demanded more vodka. Elga informed
Vladimir there was none left. The festive mood turned sour,
Vladimir accusing Elga of hiding his only source of joy. A brief
but terse argument ensued in Russian. Finally Elga stood up
and went upstairs, I thought for the evening, but within minutes she returned with an open, half-empty bottle she had
been stashing. Now he'd have to do without vodka tomorrow,
she reminded him, because liquor stores were shut on Sundays in America.

Elga disappeared. I was saddened by the episode and
asked Vladimir if he minded if I smoked; I needed my palliative. He said he didn't mind, but I felt compelled to explain I
was thinking of smoking marijuana, not tobacco. He replied
he didn't care; young men had a right to smoke reindeer dung

if they were so inclined. I lit up, he sipped, and soon we were taking turns telling each other about one childhood in great expanses of snow and another in seas of sugar cane. We described simple games we had played with friends, recalled how life seemed solidly entrenched along immutable paths until suddenly, two revolutions derailed history. At some point the conversation became monologues, one in Russian and one in Spanish, and although neither spoke the other's language we understood perfectly what each was saying, and when we finished speaking we wept.

ꙮ

Towards the end of October, I received the first registered letter ever sent me. Although the manner of delivery was very personal, the envelope contained a form letter drafted by an impersonal narrator and addressed to an abstract implied reader. But the implications were quite clear. The draft board was making it easy for me to sever my umbilical cord to academia. The National Defense fellow was to become part of the national defense. The members of the board could see through my transcript riddled with B's that my heart wasn't in the paper chase, and they were sparing me the anxiety of writing a dissertation. The members of the board may have been common folks, but they were no dummies. They knew a bogus dissertation when they saw one. They were not as easily persuaded as Congress, who had voted to spend billions blindly for the Humanities in the name of National Defense.

For the first time in my life, the possibility of going to war was real. Until then the idea of war had been, like the idea of death itself, a fascinating topic to consider from the comfort of a reading chair or the safety of the imagination. As a boy I had often pretended to be an American soldier in World War II, especially when I accompanied my father and his cronies on hunting forays to the Zapata swamps. While the hunters massacred hundreds of sitting ducks basking in the winter tropical warmth, I emptied my pellet rifle on imaginary Japs hiding in the bush. Later, as a teen-ager full of patriotic fervor trying to measure up to a grandfather who had fought alongside the Rough Riders in the Spanish War, I had gone as far as signing up for what turned out to be the Bay of Pigs invasion. Fortunately for me then, my father, the staunch anti-Communist, made sure my name was honorably deleted from the list of volunteers and put me away in a private school, well protected from the Cuban zealots who ruled Miami.

There was so much literature, great literature, inspired by the folly and grandeur of war that as a student of *belles lettres* harboring ambitions of *producing* literature, I could not help but wonder if war might not be a necessary evil for character formation, indeed a prerequisite to full manhood. Hemingway's example alone sufficed. Moreover, was my generation's reluctance to fight an "immortal war" disguised cowardice, as the hawks claimed? For whatever dark reason lurking in my subconscious, I had decided not to resist the draft board's ruling.

When Vladimir dropped by the office at the customary hour that evening, I showed him the letter and explained the contents. Seeing he was confused, I joked about going to fight the Communists in Vietnam so that we both could go back home. But he didn't see the humor. Vladimir's blue eyes turned inward. He was gone an eternity, and when he came back the fire in his pupils told me he'd been in hell.

Vladimir's visits now had one purpose, and one purpose only: To convince me that war was the most horrible thing in life, and that I should do whatever was necessary to avoid being drafted. Not that I had many options. To claim conscientious objector status would have been ludicrous for someone

who hadn't set foot in church for ten years and who was proud
of his agnosticism. There was a chance I'd fail the physical,
but I'd been a competitive swimmer and still worked out two
or three hours a week to relieve tension. Leaving the country
was totally out of the question. To gain political asylum in the
U.S., I had given up my Cuban passport and what few rights
went with it to Immigration. Without a passport, I couldn't
even cross the border to Tijuana.

Vladimir's nightly pleading began to have an effect on my
outlook. His descriptions of the horrors he had witnessed during World War II were much more graphic that the bloody
footage we saw every night on Walter Cronkite, though I had
started to watch those clips with different eyes, too. I began to
keep track of the casualties and to figure the odds of my being
one. Every day, or so it seemed, the chances improved.

I decided to tell no one else about the impending physical,
not even my family. It had been scheduled for the first week of
December. If I passed it, I could finish the semester, spend
Christmas at home, and report to the induction center for
assignment after New Year's.

What I remember most about the physical is the final
line-up to check for hernias, the rape at the end of eight hours
of torture. Two rows of about one hundred men each faced off.
We were told to drop our pants. A doctor and an assistant
began the inspection. First you were ordered to bend over,
grab your buttocks, and expose your anus. After checking for
hemorrhoids, the doctor squeezed the scrotum and asked you
to cough. This grotesque procedure could mean the difference
between life and death, between life in a wheelchair and freedom.

If I had any doubts about going to war after Vladimir's
impassioned pleas, they were shredded by the demeaning bat-
tery of tests administered by abusive, arrogant officers. I sur-

prised myself at how very consciously I objected to their
authority. I didn't believe a word they said, and above all, I
didn't want to put my life at their mercy.

One lucky fellow was found to have a hernia, but it wasn't I.

~⚭◎

The institution where I was committed after being found
mentally incompetent to stand trial for arson was located
clear across the state from the town where the university was,
three hundred miles to the west. When Vladimir and Elga
came to visit me, they kept remarking how much the landscape reminded them of the steppes. It was late winter, and
beyond the hospital fences the winter wheat was beginning to
push through the snow.

We had a happy reunion. Elga had baked me a batch of
cookies, and she had brought some nice tea that we brewed in
the kitchen. Since it was Saturday, they insisted on watching
Lawrence Welk. We even danced to the polka to the cheers of
my fellow mates who were in the rec room.

My friends had to catch the lone bus going east at eight,
so it was a short visit. We hugged and kissed Russian style,
and they promised to come back in the summer when the
wheat was ripe.

Just as they were leaving, Elga reached inside her purse
and handed me a sealed envelope. I waited until I went to bed
before opening it, expecting to find a note and a little cash to
spend at the hospital store. Instead I found a hand-written
confession, signed by Vladimir and witnessed by Elga, admitting it was he, not I, who had started the fire in the Dean's
office of the Humanities building. I was to turn it in to the
police at the end of the war or after Vladimir died, whichever
came first.

It was a true confession, but I burned it and threw the ashes out into the night.

Playa

Where he had come from, no one could ever tell me. He swept into my life suddenly and irrevocably the first night after we arrived in Varadero, one more of the many sensations that left forever their impression on me that Friday in June. My mother had sent me to bed early, but I couldn't sleep, too excited to wait for morning to plunge into that seductive sea I had seen for the first time that evening. I found myself breathing the sea air harshly, almost with violence because it was so different from the dusty burning air of the countryside. Then, trying to put myself to sleep, I set myself to counting the holes in the rectangular section of the mosquito net lit up by the street lamp. Then I heard a voice imitating a radio announcer. I lifted the mosquito net, taking care not to knock over the poles, and put my bare feet on the tile floor, which seemed to be sweating in the tropical night. Through the grating on the window I saw him under the silent stars. He was atop a beer crate that some mean people had set up for him below the almond tree next to the butcher's shop. The man was so black that the contours of his figure dissolved into the night, he a part of the night and the night a part of him. When he stopped talking, someone threatened to turn him off, so he burst into a song again or invented commercials. On other nights, he'd broadcast baseball games. Now, all the nights are one in my memory, and the echo of his voice still describes imaginary home runs that go, go, and are gone over the fence at Havana Stadium.

Who knows how many bounces he had taken, like a spinning billiard ball. All I have been able to find out is that one day he showed up at José's stand, that he ordered a cognac, and didn't have the means to pay for it.

José wasn't stingy and let it slide. So then we started talkin' to him. That day we were all gonna take three boats to Mono Grande Key, since Dominico's men had gone there and returned with a big catch of yellowtail snapper. We'd stopped off at the stand to drink some coffee before goin' down to the beach, and it was there that we met the black man, the so-called Playa, which is what he told us to call him. We immediately realized that he'd lost his marbles. We paid José what he owed and bought him two or three more drinks to free up his tongue, to see just how many screws he had loose. From the nonsense that came out of his mouth, we figured that he had escaped from the looney bin.

I didn't believe that. I preferred to believe the stories he spun in the shade of the beached boats after he woke up from a nap or after a game of dominoes. Because on the following morning, something compelled me to look for him, and I found him at the pier on 48th Street, over by El Castillito. I began to play stupidly with the wet sand, watching him over my shoulder until, realizing that I wanted to talk to him, he threw the seed of a honeyberry at my head. He laughed at his marksmanship and called to me, "Hey, you, come here."

When I got to his side, he told me, "I am Playa and you are a spoiled little rich brat."

What he said embarrassed me because it was true; at school the other boys always teased me, calling me a rich kid and saying my father was a miser who buried his money in the backyard. He must have realized that his words upset me because he started to laugh again heartily and added, "A spoiled, rich white boy, and you can see it a mile away."

I remained silent. I was about to start crying from humiliation and leave, but then he put his large hand on my shoulder to console me.

"Don't be silly, boy, I was just kidding. Come on, what's your name? Look, haven't you ever been on a boat? Let's borrow this dinghy for a little while, and I'll teach you to row."

From then on I looked for him every day at the pier by El Castillito. In time, I began to realize that he had sailed all over the world in freighters. He knew English and bits and pieces of many other languages. I bet him once that he hadn't been to Russia, but he said that, yes, he had been in Odessa. I named the most distant countries and the most exotic ports I could think of, and he confirmed that he had set foot in all of them. Thus he filled my imagination with marvellous worlds which I replayed at night while lying in bed. I began to spend very little time with my parents. At first they didn't worry, but after a few weeks, they made a point of taking me out for a walk in the evenings, either to ride the Flying Dutchman or for ice cream. I was secretive towards them, until one day at lunchtime it occurred to me to repeat what Playa had told me the previous afternoon.

"Playa says that when the war was on, he went as a cook on an English steamer that stopped in Matanzas to load sugar. He says that the waters in the North are dirty, so thick that you can't even see the bottom near the shore. And he says that at night, when he went out on deck, he was more scared of the sea serpents than of the German submarines. That he's seen enormous serpents following in the wake of the steamer, lamenting their loneliness."

That night my mother made me pray the rosary with her. Afterward, she lectured me. "Your father is very upset because you pay so much attention to that crazy black man, and you don't even show *him* any affection. You have no idea how much he loves you, the sacrifices he's made so one day you can study at the university in Havana. Therefore, from now on, I don't want you to meet that Playa. God knows what kinds of ideas he's putting into your head. If we see you with him again, we're going to forbid you to go to the beach as punishment until we return to Camagüey."

But I didn't pay any attention to them. I learned to tell lies, and instead of going to the park to roller-skate, I would slip away to José's stand or to the tavern to watch Playa play dominoes. I sat behind him and observed the ritual of his long, agile fingers as they chose the pieces one by one, turned them over, and with the white circles etched in the ebony, constructed a trap that would determine the moves of the other players. Sometimes, before going down to the beach, if he had won, he would buy me coffee at El Castillito. The bitter flavor that was forbidden to me at home, the thrill of being surrounded by fishermen who used profanities and spoke of women made me feel older, and I believed that I was beginning to decipher the mysteries of life. My parents orderly, clean world became increasing repugnant to me, whereas Playa's captivated me with the sweet honey of fiction.

One evening when he had been talking to a group of fishermen about one of his voyages, someone asked him why his name was Playa. Before responding, he kicked the sand beneath him with his heels and looked northward towards the sea as if he were searching for the answer in that neutral zone of the horizon.

"I wanted to name myself Playa because the beach is the most beautiful thing in the world. Here, the three elements— water, air, and land—come together in perfect harmony. The sea represents constant change, the earth the stability of time, and the air the change in stability."

Many fishermen laughed, not understanding him. I didn't understand him either. But I cherished his words because I always believed that they held secret meaning. For that reason more than any other, I got close to him.

Playa didn't pay any attention to the laughter. He stood up to put more strength into his words.

"When I die, I would like to be buried on the beach, like the green turtle, in the solitude of the Frenchman's Cove. I want to be buried without a coffin, so I can hear the storms and the breaking of the waves clearly. And I don't want anyone to mark the grave with a cross, so no one will bother me with their prayers or witchcraft."

The group of fishermen left, laughing at Playa's foolishness. When we were alone, he looked at me. He was sad and when he spoke to me, it was in a voice that announced the end.

"I am already tired of life. One of these days, I'll throw myself into the sea and end it all. When I was a young man I wanted to live forever, even though I wasn't afraid of death. Now I realized what a curse it would be to live forever."

"Disobedience. We already warned you once. If there's one thing that will not be tolerated in this house, it's disobedience. I have already heard enough about that loathsome black man. For now, you can't leave the house alone. Your vacation is over. Go to your room and study until dinnertime. You're going to be an upright man even if we have to enroll you in a Jesuit school."

"So your parents punished you. That doesn't surprise me. What do you say they called me, that crazy black man? Someday you'll learn that your parents can make mistakes just like anyone else. Well, why rush things if you'll discover on your own what the world is all about? But of one thing I'm sure, and that's that the world will become all screwed up. I'm not going to see it, but I've got a feeling. It's best if you go, before they catch you with me and punish you more."

❦

"Sing, Playa, sing. If you don't, we'll unplug you."

From my bed I could hear the cries of the crowd, and I couldn't understand how people could be so cruel. I didn't want to push aside the mosquito net and peep out the window to see him humilated. Since my parents had confined me to the house, the night seemed to exercise its evil influence on Playa's moods; it filled him with crazy blood. It was then that he became a toy for others to play with and for his own mind.

Later, his broadcasts ceased. The fishermen returned without him. No one escapes the wrath of the sea, that's what everyone said. That the hammerhead shark had swallowed him. That the manta ray had sucked his blood. One less crazy person to deal with, my father said.

❦

"I liked Playa all right. He was a ravin' lunatic, but he was a madman that never hurt no one. I never once saw him get violent. He knew how to do a little bit of everything, and it wasn't hard for him to make a livin'. He patched up castin' nets and traps, or he'd go down to the mangrove to make charcoal. He was a first-class cook and could've found a job in any hotel, but he said he'd had enough of cookin' on the freighters. He liked fishin' a lot, but only for the pure pleasure of it, not to make a livin'. He said that the life of a fisherman was too tough. And that ain't no lie. Look how my hands are furrowed from reeling in the lines and from unhooking the fish."

Not just his hands. The fisherman's feet didn't look like they belonged to a human being from so much walking on the coral and in the mangrove. Between his big and second toes, a deep furrow had formed. It served as a groove for fishing line when his hands were busy cutting up chum. His body was still taut, in spite of his age; his face, weathered by the salt air and the sun.

"Many fish have passed through these hands," he concluded before taking a swig from the brandy. And then he added, "I don't know why you want me to tell you all this. Anyway, there ain't no one who can raise a dead man no matter how much you talk about him. Thanks for the brandy. It's been so long since all this happened that my memory fails me, and the booze helps refresh my memory...

"It was the night of the thunderstorm. Better said, a bitch of a squall had passed through in the evening, and it kept me from goin' to Cayo Piedras as I had planned. I already had everything prepared, and it pissed me off to have to waste all that preparation. So instead, I'd gone to the tavern to gamble away the money I had left on dominoes and to wait for the rain to stop, so I could go back home. Then Playa shows up and the people start to mess with him as usual. The truth is that people are born evil. Well, it occurred to me to ask him if he wanted to go cast a line over by the rocky bottom of La Peñita. I already told you that he was always nagging me to take him fishin'. I dunno why this idea occurred to me, but when something bad's gonna happen, it will happen, no matter what you do. The evening was still sultry, even though the sea was completely smooth. But the sea, the bitch, she is a traitor; you can't trust her. So what happened is that Playa got really excited when I asked him if he wanted to go, and I gave up my seat to someone else, seeing as how I couldn't even win a stinkin' cent.... But say, at least they could bring us some more brandy, my throat is gettin' dry again.... I'm not used to talkin' so much. At sea you learn to go about silently. Out there, sometimes you don't even know if you said something or if you thought it.... I don't want to offend you or anything, but the truth is that the products of the Revolution ain't worth a damn. So why don't I leave, you ask? Don't think that at times I haven't been tempted to continue sailing north when I'm out fishin', to see if it's true what people write in the letters: that over there they've got cars and color TVs, the same people who before were dyin' of hunger here and didn't even have nothin' to wipe their asses with. But I'm too old for that now. Here I was born, and here I will be buried. So do you have anyone in your family who flew the coop, or is your whole family loyal to Fidel?... I'm sorry to hear that man, but you're not the only one who's lost his parents to El Norte....

"It'd already stopped raining and we went down to the beach. I'd left the basket with the sardines and the canteen under the bow to keep them from getting wet. So, as soon as we arrived, we shoved off. The sea was like glass, and the motor started with a crack; I've always made sure my motor starts after just one crank. I put him at the rudder and began to put things in order, to cut chum and prepare the hooks. When I finished, I took the rudder and he began to brew some coffee—that black, man-made, mean coffee. I dunno why that should be, but there are people who have a hand blessed for cookin'. He used the same kerosene burner and the same pot as I did, the same amount of sugar and coffee, but it turned out much better than mine. Go figure it out. I remember that after we drank the coffee, he began to sing I don't know what in English. He said somethin' about Jamaicans.... Was he Jamaican? Who knows. He never said where he was from.

Prob'ly he was born on a boat, like they say so many slaves were. Anyway, we went on happily towards La Peñita, calculatin' how much we'd make if by chance we caught 100 pounds of fish. A fisherman must always have hope, or he'll never catch anything....

"We'd started gettin' hungry, so we put the canteen next to the motor to reheat the food. By the time we arrived at La Peñita, we'd eaten and were ready to fish all night long. We arrived in total darkness, but in those days I had eyes like a lynx and it wasn't hard at all to find a promising bottom.... In the rock formation of La Peñita there's not much depth; we must have cast anchor at about eight fathoms. Man, I wouldn't exaggerate, in half an hour we had a big enough catch to stop and go home happy. You know how the schools of mango snapper sometimes surface, and then all Hell breaks loose. Cast the hook and reel in. Cast and reel in. There's nothin' to it but to slap a sardine, head and all, on the hook, and you'll catch one. We didn't even have time to piss. In about three hours, we already had filled more than half the barrel; two more hours like those and it'd have been to the brim. But right then, the Boss arrives. Without warning, the fish stop biting, and I says to myself: shark. We've got to get out of here. I told Playa to take in the tackle, because from now on, the shark would eat anything that bites. Anyway, we had caught more than enough, so we brought in the tackle and got ready to raise anchor.

"It was still early; I knew it even though the clouds covered the stars, so we took our time. Playa brewed another pot of coffee, we ate some guava paste on crackers, and then we lit a pair of cigars. Listen, young man, those were the good old days, poverty and all. Havin' a young body: nothing else matters. There's not much left in me now; I can feel it in my legs, which fail me when I'm out fishin'. I envy you. You're what,

about 30 now? You still have the best part of life ahead of you.
What I don't understand is why, for what fuckin' reason, you
want to know this story. Yes, you already told me that you're
a journalist, but journalists write about things that happen
now. Or don't they? After I told the police everything, I buried
it with the dead man. You'd better believe it gave me a good
scare. The authorities didn't want to believe me. The truth is,
I don't even know how it happened.... You must pardon me,
but my throat is gettin' dry again.... I hope you're not gonna
think that I'm a drunkard. I never drink to get drunk. When
my blood warms up, that's more than enough. Okay, I'll go on,
the best I can, without making anything up. This is beginning
to feel like a police interrogation. Fine. Listen, man, haven't
you ever spent a night out at sea? You don't know what you're
missin'. That night was special. I already told you that the sea
was dead calm. When the sea's like that, the night is filled
with lights. They say it's from the phosphorous. It's like every
fish you catch comes up like a sparkler. When you take it off
the hook, it leaves your hands with a greenish glow. And
when you sail, that's even more beautiful. The wake you leave
behind seems like it's on fire. That night the only thing
missin' was the stars. On the radio they talk a lot about freedom, and this and that and the other. Well, for me, all I want
is that they leave me in peace with my boat and my tackle.
They tried to put me in a fishermen's cooperative, but I'll have
none of that. I go out alone or with a mate of my choosing. Not
even if Fidel Castro himself comes to tell me to, I won't join a
cooperative. Well, enough said. Back to the story. I told you
that I like the night out at sea. Well, there's nothin' I like better than to snooze out there. Since the night was calm, I decided to turn the rudder over to Playa and take a short nap. Not
even a child could get lost; all you had to do was point the
prow at the lights of El Castillito and head in a straight line.

He got up on the poop to steer with his feet and crossed his arms. I told him to wake me up when we were about to arrive, and went to sleep. I came to when the motor stopped because it'd run out of gas, and the sudden silence didn't feel right. I said, 'What's up, Playa?' But when I straighten out I realize that I'm alone and there ain't land nowhere in sight. The sun still hadn't risen, but it was beginning to get light. I said to myself, shit, what the fuck's happened here? I started to yellin' for him, but he wasn't gonna hear no one ever again. I don't believe in witchcraft, but at that moment it seemed to me like someone had put a curse on me. Imagine, wakin' up and findin' yourself on the high seas, and without gas to boot. I took a good look at where the sun would come up and began to row for shore. Luckily, there wasn't even a breath of wind. When I arrived, already almost noon, I went and told everything to the police. They held me until the body appeared and they saw that it didn't have a mark on it. Well, let me tell you…. I already told you that he had gotten up on the poop to steer with his feet. That's somethin' we old fishermen do. What I believe is that he fell asleep and then fell into the water. I didn't hear his scream, and he got screwed. Is it possible that he threw himself into the water? Listen, that hadn't occurred to me. Could be. You already know he was crazy. Though that night he had behaved like an ordinary, common man. But when it comes to crazy people, one never knows. What's the difference; either way he's dead, just like there's no difference between a ship powered by wind and one by steam. The two sail on the same sea."

"But after three days he was resurrected. His body appeared at dawn face down, in front of the yacht club. The high tide had deposited him in the sand like a shell, and when I arrived, small waves were licking his feet.

"I stayed there until they took him away. The sea had respected him. He had all of his flesh intact. Only his skin had lost the luster of life.

"No one dared touch him until the inspector from Matanzas came. When they finally lifted him up, I could see the mask his face had imprinted on the sand. In a few minutes, the wind had erased it forever.

"Now only his bones and the memory of his voice remain. At least I was able to convince authorities to let me exhume them and bury them again where I wished. They are under an *hicaco* tree in Frenchman's Cove. May he rest in peace."

(Translated by Zhenja La Rosa)